HANG TEN FOR
DEAR LIFE!

IN DUE TIME

HANG TEN FOR DEAR LIFE!

by Nicholas O. Time

SIMON SPOTLIGHT

New York   London   Toronto   Sydney   New Delhi

SIMON SPOTLIGHT
An imprint of Simon & Schuster Children's Publishing Division
1230 Avenue of the Americas, New York, New York 10020
This Simon Spotlight hardcover edition May 2017
Copyright © 2017 by Simon & Schuster, Inc.
Text by Sheila Sweeny Higginson. Cover illustration by Stephen Gilpin.
All rights reserved, including the right of reproduction in whole or in part in any form. SIMON SPOTLIGHT and colophon are registered trademarks of Simon & Schuster, Inc. For information about special discounts for bulk purchases, please contact Simon & Schuster Special Sales at 1-866-506-1949 or business@simonandschuster.com.
Designed by Jay Colvin. The text of this book was set in Adobe Garamond Pro.
Manufactured in the United States of America 0417 FFG
10 9 8 7 6 5 4 3 2 1
ISBN 978-1-4814-9655-1 (hardcover)
ISBN 978-1-4814-9654-4 (paperback)
ISBN 978-1-4814-9656-8 (eBook)
Library of Congress Control Number 2016957834

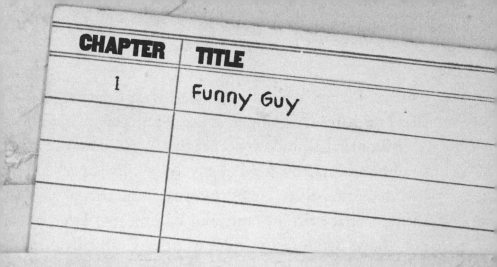

CHAPTER	TITLE
1	Funny Guy

"Pssst, hey, Maria," I whisper to the girl sitting in front of me.

Maria Malki flips her long, bouncy brown hair, then turns around and stares at me, her black eyes looking like they will shoot flames if I dare make another sound. She puts her index finger on her lips and whispers back, "Shhh, Kai!"

I twist my face so it looks like one of those super-sad clowns you see in the paintings at a mall kiosk. Maria's stony look starts to show a few cracks. Her lips turn up a teeny-tiny bit at the corners. I see a sliver of opportunity, so I decide that I'm definitely going to squeeze my way in.

Maria's a rule follower. I get that. I'm a pretty straight-and-narrow kind of guy myself. I've only had detention three times this year, and two of them weren't even my fault. But I admit that I'm not above bending the rules a little. Especially when it involves getting a laugh or two. I *live* for laughs.

The rule Maria is reminding me about is "No talking during Mr. Bodon's math class." He's pretty strict about it, and breaking it already got me the one detention that I actually deserved. But Mr. Bodon just left the room to go talk to Principal DiBella, and I desperately need to try out some new comedy material, so here goes nothing. . . .

"Hey, Maria," I whisper. "What's blue and smells like red paint?"

Maria is *not* going to break the rule and talk to me, but I can tell she wants to know the punch line when she turns around and shrugs her shoulders.

Katrina, Jaden, and Faris are sitting close by, and they're all in too.

"I don't know. What?" Faris whispers.

"Blue paint," I say matter-of-factly.

Maria drops her head on her desk and groans. My friend Matt snickers from two rows over.

"Dude, that is such a dumb joke." He laughs. "Seriously, Kai. Did you actually spend time coming up with it?"

"Did it make you laugh?" I ask.

"Well, sure," Matt says. "Because it's soooo dumb."

"Doesn't matter," I say. "If it made you laugh, it worked."

Maria's head is still on her desk, but I think I can hear the faintest sound of a giggle. Success!

Mr. Bodon comes back into the room and starts writing math problems on the board.

"You have ten minutes to complete these problems," he announces to the class. "If you need help, come see me in the consulting corner."

Mr. Bodon's "consulting corner" is a card table with two chairs that he put in one corner of the classroom. It's kind of cheesy, but he's actually one of our coolest teachers. I start writing down the problems he's written on the board and

I can tell that I'm going to need some consulting with problems two, three, and four.

I finish writing the problems down and I'm just about to close my notebook and head to the card table when a folded piece of paper lands on my desk. I open it and see that Maria has written the formula for figuring out the perimeter and area of quadrilateral shapes on it. Now I can do all the problems on my own. Sweet!

It's probably a good time to explain that Maria Malki has been sitting in front of me for five years now. We went to the same elementary school, and since my last name is Mori, alphabetical-order seating has pretty much doomed us to being friends. She knows that I never remember to bring my sheet of math formulas, even though I'm supposed to. I know she's one of the best students, and artists, in our grade.

I guess "doomed" isn't really the right word, though, because even though we're really different, like, opposite-ends-of-the-spectrum different (and I'd never admit this to my guy friends like Matt), I think Maria is kind of cool, for a strictly-following-the rules-kind-of girl, that is.

Thanks to Maria, I finish the math problems in four minutes, so I have six minutes to let my mind wander. I should probably start working on a new joke, but I'm not really in the mood, so I just look down at the floor in front of me, which is where Maria's stack of books and her backpack are. Maybe her books will inspire me.

Another thing about Maria: She is obsessed with animals. I've never seen her room, but I'm going to guess she has posters of kittens and tigers and dolphins plastered everywhere. She's probably drawn a lot of them too, because she's a pretty amazing artist. Her backpack is covered with bubble-pen drawings of animals that she did herself, and it actually looks like something you could buy in a store.

I don't even realize it, but while I'm looking at the backpack, I start doodling in my math notebook. Inspired by Maria, I guess. Stick figures are about the best I can do, but I get distracted pretty easily. Doodling helps me focus when my brain would rather be somewhere else. I start with some swirly waves and then add some dolphin fins and starfish, simple stuff. I get so absorbed in it that I'm totally startled when the end-of-period bell rings. I jump up and accidentally flip my notebook off my desk.

Maria is already packing up her stuff, so she grabs my notebook and sneaks a peek at my doodles. How totally embarrassing! She's a real artist. I'm a . . . a doodler. And not even a decent doodler. Ugh. She's totally going to laugh at me. And not the kind of laugh I'm looking for.

"Here, Kai," Maria says, handing me the notebook.

Wow, not even a smirk. Amazing!

Then she quietly zippers her backpack and starts to head off.

"Uh, thanks, Maria," I call after her. "See you at lunch!"

Maria turns around and doesn't even lift her head when she says, "If you really care about ocean creatures, you should come to the Be the Change club meeting later."

"What was that about?" Matt Vezza asks, shoving me in the back. "See you at lunch, Maria! Is there something you're not telling me, Kai?"

"What? No, nothing!" I protest. "She just

helped me, so I figured I had to be nice. I'm not rude, Matt!"

"Of course you're not." Faris Riley laughs. "Just ignore him."

Faris turns to Matt and says, "Come on, like Kai would *ever* like Maria! She's so quiet—and he's so loud!"

Matt laughs. "Yeah, you're right. Kai would just bulldoze every conversation."

"Gee, thanks, guys," I say. "It's nice to know you really appreciate me."

"Aw, don't take it personally," Faris says. "We love you. You're our favorite class clown ever!"

I should be more upset than I am, but I'm not really paying attention to them anymore. I'm thinking about how I'm going to come up with some kind of a sea creature joke before the Be the Change club meeting.

When I find Maria in the cafeteria after school, she and Jada Reese are waving their hands while they talk. It's a girl thing. I decide to watch them for a few minutes. I like to study people's expressions and gestures so I can mimic them closely. It helps with my comedy routine. Like, watching Maria and Jada right now, I'm pretty sure I can get a girl impression down pretty perfectly. I move a little closer so I can hear what they're saying. They're both too focused on the conversation to even notice me.

"We could have a bake sale to help a local shelter," Maria says. "Or maybe a poster contest to show why it's important to help save the animals of the rain forest? Or . . ."

"Those are great ideas, Maria," Jada says. "But right now we're all tied up with toy drive for the children's hospital. I don't have any time to spare."

"Well, if you start an animal-charity subgroup," I suggest, "you won't have to spare any time. Someone else will."

Jada and Maria whip their heads around and stare at me.

"When did you join the club?" Jada wonders aloud.

"Oh, I asked Kai to stop by," Maria said. "The more the merrier, right?"

"Right." Jada laughs. "So are you going to lead this subgroup, Kai?"

"Um, I think that sounds like a job for someone a lot more together than I am," I admit. "Like Maria?"

"I'm in," Maria says.

"That would be great if you can to take total charge of it, Maria," Jada says. "I have so much to do already."

"I can," Maria says. "With Kai's help, of course."

"Of course." I laugh, hoping my cheeks aren't turning red. "But I have to go now. I've got plans . . . you know . . . um . . . this thing . . ."

"Right," Maria says. "Why don't you just stop by my house when you're done and we can brainstorm some ideas?"

"Sorry, I think this, um, thing is going to take a while," I say cryptically. "Can we meet tomorrow? At the library maybe?"

"Sure," Maria says. "I'll make a list of some ideas tonight and bring them with me."

"Great!" Jada says, already whirling off to talk to another group of kids. "Good luck, you guys."

"See you tomorrow, Kai," Maria says, smiling.

My eyes lock in on her teeth. They're perfectly white and straight. I've never actually noticed that before, and it makes me remember my mouth full of metal braces. I put my hand over them and mumble, "Bye."

I finish up my homework quickly that afternoon. Writing comes really easily to me, so the five-page social studies paper that everyone's been complaining about takes me only about an hour to finish, and then I spend another half hour on math and science. Then it's time for my real homework. Comedy!

I entered a comedy contest that WKBL, our local radio station, is running. I have to prepare a five-minute stand-up routine to perform at the Smoke Eater's Jamboree (a festival to raise money for our fire department). I'm doing a "Did You Ever Wonder?" theme. It's full of lines like, "Did you ever wonder why we sing 'Take Me Out to the Ball Game' when we're already there?"

My mom is the funniest person I know—no joke!—and she's been helping me get ready, but I want to write at least another page of jokes. That's the thing about comedy. You have to write a lot more material than you need, so that you can cut the stuff that doesn't really fly and keep only the best stuff. I'm not sure about the "Take Me Out to the Ball Game" line, but I'm going to try it out and see if it makes anyone laugh. Mom first, of course, because I know she won't let me embarrass myself out there. Besides being funny, she's brutally honest too.

Dad's the first to get home, and before he even says hello to me he turns on the rice cooker in the kitchen. My family's originally from Japan, so rice is part of dinner pretty much every night. Our rice cooker has probably made enough rice to fill one of the Great Lakes.

Pretty soon Mom's home, and I run some of my new routine by her.

"Did you ever wonder what it would sound like if Kermit the Frog rapped?" I ask.

"Not really. Why?" Mom asks.

I do my best impression of Kermit the Rapper.

"Cute," Mom says. "But don't you think the Chipmunks would be funnier?"

Right! My Chipmunk impression is killer. I start to rap again, but this time with a super-squeaky voice.

Dad snorts and Mom cracks up.

"Do I know funny?" she asks.

"You know funny, Mom," I agree.

Dinner's ready and the table's all set when my big sister, Yumi, and her best friend, Val, come bouncing through the door. They're on the high school gymnastics team, so when I say bounce, I mean it literally.

"How's good old Sands Middle School?" Val asks, and rolls her eyes.

"Probably the same as when you went there," I reply.

"I'm sorry," Val says.

"It's okay," I say.

Yumi and Val start talking about this boy they know who used to go to middle school with them.

"Have you seen Troy Mendez?" Yumi asks.

"Yes!" Val screams. "When did he get so cute?"

"Does he still have braces?" I ask.

Yumi and Val both look at me like I have six heads.

"What?" they say.

"Does he still have braces?" I repeat. "I mean, can he be cute with braces?"

"No. He got them off last year," Val says.

"Why, are you hoping someone thinks you're cute with braces?" Yumi teases.

"No. I . . . I was just . . . um . . . wondering," I stammer.

Thankfully, the phone rings and interrupts our conversation. It's Oji-san, otherwise known as my uncle Kenji. He lives in Honolulu, Hawaii, which is where my mom grew up. Oji-san is a lawyer, just like my mom, and once they get started talking, there's no stopping them. We finish dinner and clean up and Mom is still on the phone, asking a ton of questions all about her brother's new case in Hawaii's environmental court.

I head up to my room to escape from Yumi and Val, and check my cell phone. (We're not allowed to have phones at the dinner table—strict Mori-family rule.) There's a text message from a strange number. I tap on it and see: *Hey! Library tmrw still cool?*

It's Maria! How did she even get my number?

I agree to meet her—of course—but figure I should do some research before I go to bed, so that I'm totally prepared for our meeting. I start digging around Oji-san's cases with the environmental court, because I know he's done some work getting wildlife protection there. It's kind of a family tradition, actually. Baba, my grandmother, is a marine biologist. She's studied the breeding cycles of the local fish schools and helped make sure that endangered species weren't overfished. Maria is going to be soooo impressed!

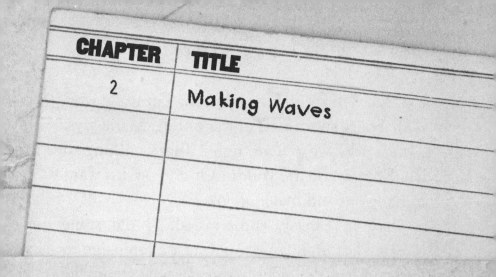

CHAPTER	TITLE
2	Making Waves

"What do you call a fake noodle?" I ask Maria when I see her in the library after school the next day.

"I don't know," Maria says.

"An impasta!" I laugh.

Maria does not. Guess it's time to cross that joke off the list.

"Why do sharks live in salt water?" I try again. No answer.

"Because pepper makes them sneeze!" I snort. Still no laugh. Wow.

"Kai, I'm sorry, but right now I'm really worried about the animals of the world," Maria says. "That's why we're here, right? That's nothing to laugh about. So are you in? Or do you just want to hang out and make up jokes?"

"I'm in," I say, embarrassed. "I did some research last night. We could start a campaign to let people in the neighborhood know about the dangers of using pesticides in their garden. Or we could do a car wash to raise money for a local animal shelter."

"I like those ideas," Maria said. "But let's hit the books. I want to do something that could be really effective, not just something that looks good on the surface or that only helps for a short time."

"Good idea," I say. "I'm sure Ms. Tremt will know just which books will help."

"You're right," Maria says. "Of course she will!"

Ms. Tremt is our librarian. She has to be the best middle-school librarian on the planet, seriously. Our library isn't new and it doesn't have a ton of books, but if you're looking for a book—

any book—Ms. Tremt always seems to be able to find it. Her book-finding ability is pretty extraordinary, just like her scarves. Actually, her scarves are a little wacky, but I kind of like them. I've been thinking it would be fun to borrow one and try out a Ms. Tremt impression. I wonder if it would make Maria laugh. Probably not at the moment.

"Hello, Kai," Ms. Tremt says when we walk to the circulation desk. "Greetings, Maria. What can I do for you today?"

"Hi, Ms. Tremt," Maria says. "Kai and I are working on a new project for the Be the Change club. We want to do something animal-related. But we want it to really make a difference. So that's why we're here. Research!"

"Intriguing," Ms. Tremt says. "I'd love to help, but right now I'm in the middle of something. Why don't you get started and I'll be right back."

Maria starts pulling books while I log in to the computer. Before I even get to typing words into the search engine, Maria plops down next to me. She lets out a long sigh. It sounds so sad.

"We really have to do something, Kai," Maria says seriously as she reads from a book. "Did you know that almost three million dogs and cats are put to sleep every year because they don't get matched to a home?"

"I didn't know that," I say. "That's horrible. What can we do?"

"Your idea to raise money for a local shelter was good," Maria says. "But what else can we do?"

"It says here that pets that are more attractive are more likely to be adopted," I read.

"Hmmm. Maybe we could learn how to groom them," Maria says.

"Training is also pretty important," I continue. "Maybe that's something we can learn to do too. I bet that would help."

"I think we're on to something," Maria says. "Keep reading."

Maria leans in to get a better look at the screen, and when she does, her knee bumps into my knee. It feels a little like an electric shock, and I jump in my seat.

"Oops, sorry," Maria says. "Did you get hurt playing baseball?"

"Something like that," I lie. More like a bad case of Maria-itis.

"Hey, Maria," I say. "What did one knee bone say to the other knee bone?"

"Sorry for bumping into you?" Maria guesses.

"Nope." I laugh. "Let's get out of this joint."

There it is again . . . Maria's smile. I have to look away and pretend I'm reading the computer screen so Maria doesn't think I'm staring at her all googly-eyed or something.

Ms. Tremt suddenly appears out of nowhere, and behind her is an old guy wearing glasses, a red wool cap, and a denim shirt.

"Let'z get out of zis joint!" He chuckles with a French accent, quoting my punch line. "That'z funny!"

"This is my friend Jeek," Ms. Tremt says. "He's an animal lover too."

Jeek points to the cat and dog pictures on the computer screen.

"The animals I take care of are not so furry." He laughs.

"Jeek is a scuba diver," Ms. Tremt explains. "Among other things."

"Really?" I ask. "My baba dives. I mean, my grandma. She's retired now, but she was a marine biologist."

"What is her name?" Jeek asks.

"Ayumi," I say. "Ayumi Tanaka. But she lives far away . . . in Hawaii."

"Oh yes, I know Ayumi," Jeek says. "Lovely woman. Strong diver."

"You do?" I gasp. "That's amazing! I'll have to tell her I met you."

"That's probably not a great idea," Ms. Tremt says, looking concerned.

"Why not?" I wonder.

"Oh, you know, secret diving code of silence and all," Jeek says with a wink.

"Really?" I say. "Baba never mentioned that before."

"Because it ees a secret." Jeek laughs. I do too.

"Nice to meet you, Jeek," Maria says. "Our problem right now is trying to figure out what our small group can do to make a real difference for animals."

"I like the way you think," Jeek tells her. "First you must identify the problem. Then explore simple ways that you can help solve it. Even if you can't solve it completely, there are things you can do as a start."

"Yes, that's what we're thinking too," Maria says. "We have a few ideas."

"Excellent," Jeek says. "Now, listen. This is very important: You must find ways to let people know why you're doing what you're doing. It's important to make a difference. But people must know why *they* should care to make a difference too. People protect what they love."

Maria starts to write frantically in her notebook. She is looking at Jeek like he's more than just some French friend of Ms. Tremt's.

"How do you do that?" Maria asks.

"I show them," Jeek says. "I take them to places they may never go before, under the sea. I film when I dive so I can show everyone the beauty that is hidden there, so they will care about it just as much as I do.

"I am just one small man," Jeek continues. "But I have been able to make a significant difference. There are two of you, and you are young and strong. Just think what you can do."

This Jeek guy is pretty inspiring, I have to say. It makes me want to get to work—*now*!

Our work, and our conversation, is put on hold, though, when we hear a loud crash come from the other side of the library.

The largest human I have ever seen in real life comes barreling toward us. Every muscle in his body looks like it's ready to explode. A large vein that runs down his forehead is pulsating. This dude is pumped!

I can see a lot of those muscles because the guy isn't wearing a shirt, just a fur piece thrown over one shoulder. He has three leather belts strapped around his waist, and he is wearing pants and fur-lined boots.

Ms. Tremt looks at Jeek cautiously as the guy continues to charge toward us.

Jeek takes off his cap as he bows deeply to the guy. I'm amazed at how calm Jeek is.

"Bertrand, *mon ami,* how are you?" Jeek greets the hulk. "It's been . . . what, a thousand years since we last saw each other?"

"*Hitir konungrinn Oláfr,*" the hulk growls.

"*Oui, oui,*" Jeek replies, patting the guy on his

back. "Let's go inside and catch up, shall we? We don't want to interrupt the library with our loud seafaring tales."

Jeek turns to us. "I'd introduce you to my colleague Bertrand, but he doesn't speak much English."

"*He's* a marine biologist?" Maria says disbelievingly. "He looks like a Viking!"

"And it didn't sound like he was speaking French, either," I add.

"Silly ones." Jeek laughs, but then he looks at Ms. Tremt a bit nervously. "What would a Viking be doing in your library? Bertrand and I are heading off to a marine biology convention nearby. He's a bit of a—how do you say?—a character; he always loves to surprise other biologists by showing up in crazy costumes. And when he gets into costume, he goes all out. We just stopped by to see our old friend Valerie first."

"There's a marine biology convention nearby?" I ask. "We're nowhere near the ocean."

"Did I say it was nearby?" Jeek asks, smiling. "Spending time with Valerie ees always worth a side trip, of course."

"Oh, Jeek," Ms. Tremt says, blushing. "You're such a charmer."

Bertrand, aka hulking he-man, looks confused, and like he's getting a little antsy.

"As much as I'd love to spend the whole day with you two, I think we'd better get you back now," Ms. Tremt continues. "Time is running short."

"Ah, yes," Jeek says. "Time, she waits for no man. This is very true."

Jeek turns to me and lowers his glasses.

"A question for you, young man," he says. "What is a shark's favorite kind of sandwich?"

"Huh?" I ask, confused.

"Ze peanut butter and jellyfish." Jeek laughs.

Ms. Tremt hustles Jeek and Bertrand away from us while Maria and I crack up.

"Check this out, Kai," Maria says when they're out of sight.

She types "Jacques Cousteau" into the search engine and clicks "Images." A face that looks exactly like the man who was just in the library fills the screen.

"I thought 'Jeek' looked familiar," Maria says. "And then when he said 'People protect what they

24

love,' I remembered reading that quote last Earth Day, and it was from Jacques Cousteau.

"But it can't possibly be him," Maria continues. "He died in 1997."

"Weird," I say. "Maybe Ms. Tremt is planning to surprise us with some historical presentation."

"That would be cool," Maria says. "And it would explain Bertrand. I don't really believe that whole marine biology convention story."

"I know. Me neither," I add. "I think they're a sign."

"Of what?" Maria wonders.

"A sign that our first project should be about ocean life," I reply. "Something that would make my grandmother proud."

I type "Ayumi Tanaka" and "marine biologist" into the search engine, and Baba pops up. Maria clicks on an article she wrote about an endangered species of fish.

"She's amazing!" Maria gushes as she grabs my arm and shakes me. "You're so lucky!"

I feel pretty lucky at the moment.

"My mom's pretty cool too," I say. "She's super funny."

"Oh, that's where you get it from," Maria teases.

"You can meet her if you want," I say, surprising myself. "I mean, you could come over later and we could work on the project."

"I'd love that!" Maria says. "But we'd better get going, because I won't be able to come over if I don't get started on my homework right away. That math packet Mr. Bodon gave us is *huge*!"

"I know." I sigh. "I've been trying not to think about it. Text me when you're done and I'll figure out when's a good time to come over."

"Sounds like a plan," Maria says.

"By the way, how *did* you get my phone number?" I ask.

"Oh, a good friend of yours thought you might want me to have it." Maria smiles.

Wait till I see Faris! My man!

Maria and I are walking through the door when Ms. Tremt calls after us.

"Kai!" she calls. "I have something important to ask you!"

"Tomorrow, Ms. Tremt," I shout back. "I'll be back tomorrow, I promise."

• • •

I made another promise earlier today. I promised Mom I'd clean up all my sports equipment in the garage after school. What was I thinking?

I grab my muddy cleats and start banging them together to get the dirt out, then use a wire brush to get in all the nooks and crannies. I put them in one of the shoe racks by the door that leads into the house. We have two shoe racks—one for outside shoes, one for slippers. We never wear outside shoes in the house. I don't even want to imagine my dad's reaction if he saw me wearing sneakers inside. He's a bit of a neat freak. I think his head would explode if he saw me wandering around the house in my muddy, grimy sneakers.

I open my baseball bag and find a nice collection of empty sports drink bottles. I put them in the recycling bin, then clean up the bag and put it on the shelf over the shoe rack. There are all kinds of balls, bats, helmets, and pads scattered around the garage, so I start picking them up and putting them into bins.

When Mom pulls into the driveway and sees

me, she has a big smile on her face.

"Kai-chan!" Mom says. "What happened here? You did this all on your own and I didn't see anything strange in the sky on the drive home."

"What are you talking about?" I ask her.

"You know, like flying pigs." She laughs.

"Very funny." I snicker. "How was work today?"

"Oh, you know, the usual," she says. "Lots of reading. Lots of writing. Lots of talking."

"Right," I say. "Hey, I was wondering about Oji-san. What were you talking about the other night? It sounded like a new case."

"Oh yeah, he's working on a big case to protect the waters around the Hawaiian island of Molokai from overfishing," Mom says.

"Is it a big problem?" I ask.

"Well, it seems like it might be. Some populations of fish are in danger of disappearing from the area," Mom explains. "The local fishermen rely on them to feed their families."

"Wow," I say. "Is there something we can do?"

"Kai-chan." Mom laughs. "Are you showing your mother's legal tendencies? And what's with the sudden interest in Hawaii? You haven't talked about it since last time we visited Baba."

"I'm working on a new project with one of the kids from school," I tell her. "We want to help protect animals. So when I heard you talking the other night, it got me thinking."

"Oh, then you really should look more into your great-great-aunt Akemi," Mom tells me. "Or maybe she's your great-great-great-aunt? I can never get that straight."

"Who's she?" I wonder.

"Hold on a minute," Mom says. "I may have something for you."

Mom goes to the corner of the garage that is filled with plastic storage bins and moves them around until she finds the one she's looking for. FAMILY HISTORY is written in marker on the side of the bin.

Mom lifts the lid off the bin and pulls out two plastic storage bags. Inside each bag is an ancient-looking notebook. Mom hands one of the bags to me.

"Akemi was the first person in my family to move from Japan to Hawaii," Mom explains.

"Cool," I say, looking at the Japanese writing on the cover. I can tell it says "Akemi Takahashi." Japanese writing is formed by kanji, or calligraphy pictures that you read. Mom and Dad made me go to Japanese school on Saturdays ever since kindergarten, but once I started playing sports they let me switch to online classes. I'm pretty good at reading, writing, and speaking Japanese actually. I'm almost ready to take the high school proficiency test.

Anyway, because Japanese names are made of pictures, they all have special meanings. Depending on which kanji is used, the name can mean different things. My name, Kai, is written with the kanji meaning "ocean." That kanji is made up of two parts. The left side is the character for "water" and the right side is for "mother." Interesting, right?

The two kanji for Akemi mean "bright" and "beautiful." The Takahashi kanji means "tall bridge."

"Do you have any pictures of her?" I ask Mom. "Was she really bright and beautiful?"

"Oh, I don't know," Mom says. "I don't

remember ever seeing a picture. We can ask Baba
next time we call her."

"Okay," I say. "But what does my great-great-
great-aunt have to do with animals?"

"Read and find out," Mom says. "After you
do your homework, of course."

"Of course," I reply. "Oh and, Mom?"

"Yes," Mom says.

"Is it okay if that friend comes over after dinner to work on the project?"

"Sure," Mom says. "What's his name?"

"Maria," I mumble as I race to my room.

"KAI MORI!" I hear my mom call. "Get
back here! Who's Maria? Do I know her? How
long have you been friends?"

"Later, Mom!" I yell as I close my bedroom
door. I'm not ready to answer my mom's questions. She'll meet Maria soon enough.

I send Maria a text message and tell her to
come over at seven. I know I should start plowing
through the math packet, but Akemi's journals
are sitting on my bed calling to me. I carefully
take one out of the plastic bag, hold it up to my
nose and sniff. It doesn't smell how I expect it to

smell. It's a little musty, sure, but it also smells like forest mixed with ocean water. The pages seem really fragile and I'm a little worried about turning them, but what good is preserving a journal in a plastic bag if it never gets read? So I start reading.

My eyes glance over the page. Akemi's calligraphy is neat and almost perfectly formed, but I can't read Japanese nearly as quickly as I read English, so I just try to get an overview of what she's saying. It's sad. Really sad. She's just a teenage girl, and she's totally alone. So even though she writes a lot about how beautiful the island is, and all the amazing wildlife she sees, she sounds super homesick.

Akemi also works harder than anyone I've ever met. She lives and works on a sugar plantation. She wakes up at four a.m., before the sun rises, and by six she's working in the field, planting, watering, and loading sugarcane. She only gets a thirty-minute break for lunch, and her workday ends at four thirty p.m. All that for just six dollars a month!

I could keep reading all night, but I know I have to get the math done before Maria comes, so I dive into the packet. I'm on the last problem when Yumi knocks on my door and tells me it's time for dinner. I shove scoops of rice and salmon into my mouth, then devour a whole bowl of mushrooms.

"Too hungry for jokes tonight?" Yumi says snarkily.

"Something like that," I mumble.

"Kai's having a *friennnnd* come over after dinner," Mom says.

She drags out the word "friend" in a sing-songy way so that Yumi and Dad know right away it's not just any friend—it's a girl.

"Ooooh, who is she?" Yumi asks.

"A *friend*," I say. "Just a friend. You don't know her."

Just then the doorbell rings, and I rush to get the door before Yumi can. I invite Maria inside and quickly introduce her to my family, but I don't give her time to face the interrogation I know they'd like to start.

"We've got a lot of work to do," I say. "So we'll be in Mom's office if you need us."

I get Maria settled and then run up to my bedroom to get Akemi's journals.

"These are so cool," Maria says. "You know, Kai, since you have a family connection, maybe our project should be related to ocean life. Maybe your uncle could help us."

"I'm sure he will," I tell her. "My mom talks to him every week."

I sit next to Maria and tell her what it says on the first few pages of Akemi's journal. Maria's hair smells oceany too. She must use some special shampoo or conditioner. I know she's talking about some ideas for projects, but I'm having a hard time concentrating on what she's saying, mostly because her hair is close enough for me to smell, and it smells so good.

"Hold on," I say, as I go into Mom's desk and get a notebook and pen. "Let me write that down."

We talk a lot, and write a lot, and before I know it Mom's peeking her head into the room.

"Kai-chan, it's eight thirty," Mom says. "I'll drive Maria home, so start finishing up."

Mom leaves and Maria is looking at me and smiling.

"Kai-chan?" she says. "Cute. I like it."

I know there's no hope for my face right now. I'm sure it's as red as Rudolph the Reindeer's nose. Maria doesn't seem to mind.

I come along as Mom drives Maria home, and I don't even mind when Mom asks me some questions about her on the way back. I mean, Mom can be relentless when she starts asking questions—it's the whole lawyer thing—but she's also a good listener. And that's good, since I can't really talk to any of my friends about Maria. They'd never let me live it down. I tell my mom Maria is smart and kind and laughs at my jokes (most of the time). Mom doesn't say much. She just smiles and nods.

Back at home, I hop into bed and try to work on some comedy lines, but my mind is racing and I have a hard time focusing on the funny. I spot Akemi's journals and decide that they would make the perfect bedtime story. They do.

I made a promise to Ms. Tremt, so heading up to the library is the first thing on my mind when I wake up in the morning. I hear banging and other strange noises when I get to the library door, so I'm pretty sure Ms. Tremt came in early too. The rumor around school is that she never leaves, that there's a secret room behind the library. But that's ridiculous.

"Morning, Ms. Tremt," I call when I walk in. "Hello?"

Ms. Tremt pops up from behind a tall wall of

bookshelves. She's holding a broom, and it looks like there might be some kind of cage on the floor next to her.

"Good morning, Kai," Ms. Tremt says distractedly. "Did you need something?"

"I needed to apologize for yesterday," I start to say, and then I get distracted by the scurrying sound coming from behind the bookshelf. Maybe a mouse?

I walk closer to Ms. Tremt, who is holding the broom now like she's trying to defend a goal and stop me from seeing what's back there.

More scurrying sounds. Definitely not a mouse.

I look past Ms. Tremt, and that's when a brown furry creature starts hissing from the corner.

"What in the world?!" I yell. "Ms. Tremt, is that a Triconodon? We just studied them in my science class!"

"A small prehistoric mammal with long canine teeth and powerful jaws?" Ms. Tremt gasps. "Why would I have a dangerous creature like that in here, Kai Mori?"

"Um, I don't know," I reply. "Especially considering that there haven't been any on the planet in millions of years!"

"Yes, exactly." Ms. Tremt laughs nervously. "That merely appears to be a Triconodon. In reality, it's a new robot that Jay, Grace, and Morgan built for their robotics team. I'm just having a little trouble turning it off at the moment."

"A furry robot?" I ask disbelievingly. "Are you sure you're okay?"

"To be honest, Kai, at this moment, everything is not quite 'okay,'" Ms. Tremt admits. "But in due time, it will be."

Very cryptic, Ms. Tremt. Is this some kind of 4-D chess move?

"I've got this covered, Kai," Ms. Tremt says. "I'd appreciate it if you could come back and see me later."

"Sure," I say.

"But you can do me one favor," Ms. Tremt adds. "If you run into a man wearing green gloves, please walk in the opposite direction."

"You got it, Ms. Tremt," I agree. "I'll see you later."

A furry robot that looks like a prehistoric creature in the school library is definitely hard to believe, but what's even more unbelievable is that Mr. Bodon is nowhere to be seen when I get to math class. There's a substitute teaching the class today, and he doesn't even know about the monster math packet we all did for homework last night. I spent so much time on that homework and now it's not even going to be checked. What a waste!

As more kids come in and see the sub, the room fills with sounds of groans and complaints. Middle-school students are a tough crowd. If this sub doesn't want to lose the class completely before the bell rings, he'd better do something. Now. But he doesn't seem to care about anyone talking, so maybe this is just going to be free time. That would be cool.

I tap Maria on the back to see if I can get her to break Mr. Bodon's no-talking rule, considering he's not in charge of the class today. Just then, though, the sub turns around and holds his index finger to make a "sh" sign. And the thing is, this sub, well . . . HE'S WEARING GREEN GLOVES!!!

I gasp.

"Do you know him?" Maria whispers.

"No . . . not really . . . It's just that . . . well," I hesitate.

"What???" Maria asks urgently.

"I'll tell you later," I say. "Library. After school. Okay?"

"Deal," Maria says.

The sub introduces himself to the class: Mr. Tempo. The green gloves aren't the strangest thing about Mr. Tempo. Not by a long shot.

He draws a clock and a calendar page on the board.

"Today's lesson will be about the math of time telling," Mr. Tempo explains.

Nora's hand shoots into the air. She's one of the best math students in our class.

"Are you sure you have the correct lesson plan?" Nora asks. "We haven't done a lesson on time since second grade. Mr. Bodon has been teaching us geometry for the past month."

"I'm sure that this is *my* lesson plan," Mr.

Tempo says. "So it is indeed correct."

He starts to write some dates on the board.

July 4, 1951

June 1, 1977

July 16, 1969

I see Matt whip his head around to quickly scan the room. Then he stares straight ahead, like he's frozen or something. It looks as weird as it sounds. Mr. Tempo walks down the row of desks and taps his green-gloved finger on Matt's desk.

"Can anyone tell me the numerical significance of these dates?" Mr. Tempo asks. "Does anyone see a pattern?"

Maria raises her hand.

"We'd need some more information to figure that out," she says. "There doesn't seem to be an obvious pattern."

"Correct," Mr. Tempo says. "If the pattern were obvious, I would have already figured it out by myself."

I raise my hand.

"Aren't teachers supposed to have the answers to all the problems?" I ask. "So you can show us how they work?"

"Nonsense," Mr. Tempo says. "No one has *all* of the answers."

Then he starts walking up and down the rows and looking into each of our eyes.

"Now, back to the problem at hand," Mr. Tempo says. "Does *anyone* see a pattern here?"

Of course, none of us do. Kids are starting to put their heads down on their desk because they can't stop giggling. This is the weirdest math class ever!

I'm starting to feel kind of funny, too. I raise my hand.

"How do you know if your clock is crazy?" I ask Mr. Tempo.

"What is this question?" Mr. Tempo asks. "Is there some chaos theory involved here?"

"I don't know what chaos theory is. This is just a simple question," I repeat. "How do you know if your clock is crazy?"

"How?" Matt yells out.

"It goes, 'Cuckoo!'" I say.

There are a few groans and a bunch of giggles. Mr. Tempo looks like steam might come out of his ears.

"Okay, I can see you'll be no help with the pattern," Mr. Tempo says. "What about these dates? Are they significant to anyone?"

I watch Matt shrug his shoulders and shake his head as if to say, *Who, me? Nah*, while Mr. Tempo glares at him.

I raise my hand again.

"Mr. Tempo, why are Saturday and Sunday the strongest days?" I ask.

"Ah, a fabric-of-time question," Mr. Tempo said. "I was unaware that some days are stronger than others."

"Yes," I reply. "Because all the other days are 'weak' days."

More groans. More giggles. Maria even turns around and gives me a high five.

Everyone loves it. The class starts chanting, "Kai, Kai, Kai, Kai."

"What did the digital clock say to its mother?" I ask.

43

"What?" everyone asks.

"Look, Ma, no hands!" I answer.

Mr. Tempo slams a math book on his desk.

"Insolence!" he says. "I will be reporting you all to the principal!"

He storms out of the room. The door slams behind him. The classroom is dead silent for a few seconds. We're all shocked—and a little scared. Principal DiBella is not going to be happy about this.

The whole class is sitting like statues in our seats now. We're waiting for the principal to come and read us the riot act. But it never happens. We just wait and wait and then the bell rings and we all quietly pack up our stuff and head to our next class.

"Dude, what was that?" I whisper to Faris.

"Totally comedy genius!" Faris whispers back. "Nice going, Kai!"

"I just hope we don't get a whole-class detention," Maria adds.

Everyone from my math class seems on edge the rest of the day. I've never heard the cafeteria so quiet during lunch. At the end of the day I

44

pass by Ms. DiBella in the hallway. I figure I'll take a chance and test the waters, so I nod at her and say hello.

"Hello, Kai," Ms. DiBella says back cheerfully. "How's Yumi?"

"She's doing great," I reply. "She loves high school."

Faris grabs me by the shirt when I walk by his locker a few steps later.

"No detention?" he whispers.

"Seems that way," I whisper back. "I don't think she'd be that cheerful if Mr. Tempo talked to her. Remember how angry she got just because we sat in the wrong seats when we had the sub last fall?"

"I remember," Faris says. "My parents punished me on top of detention when they got Ms. DiBella's letter!"

"Have you seen Mr. Tempo since math class?" I ask. "I wonder where he went."

"I haven't," Faris said. "I heard there was a different sub for Mr. Bodon's last period."

"I guess we got lucky, then," I say. "That's a relief."

I head to the library after I say good-bye to Faris. Maria is already sitting at the computer, doing research. I wave to her but then head over to Ms. Tremt, just to give her the heads-up about Mr. Green Gloves.

"Interesting," Ms. Tremt says. "So Tim Raveltere was your substitute teacher today."

"Oh no, wrong guy," I tell her. "Our sub was named Mr. Tempo."

Ms. Tremt laughs. "Of course he was. How obvious!"

I have *no* idea what she's talking about.

"Kai, I need to talk to you privately," Ms. Tremt says. "Follow me."

I follow Ms. Tremt into a room at the back of the library. I never actually knew the room existed, and it makes me wonder if those rumors about Ms. Tremt living here are true. But there isn't a bed or a couch or a TV or anything like that in here. Just one book, on a wooden table. It is a pretty ridiculously cool-looking book, though. And it's shimmering as if it's been touched by magic dust.

Ms. Tremt holds her hand out as if she's a

game-show hostess presenting a prize.

"Kai, may I present *The Book of Memories*," she says.

"Is it your family memories?" I ask. "Because my mom just gave me my great-great-great-aunt's journals, and I just started reading them, and—"

"No, Kai," Ms. Tremt interrupts. "This book doesn't belong to me or my family. I can't tell you whose memories are in there. You'll have to find that out for yourself."

"Ah, got it," I said. "Like a special reading project just for me."

Ms. Tremt laughs. "Something like that, Kai," she says. "But the project will involve a lot more than reading."

"Do I have to write a report, too?" I groan. "Because I have a lot of homework tonight."

"No. There is no report writing," Ms. Tremt says. "*The Book of Memories* is an adventure project. You may choose a friend or two to explore it with you. But they have to be here with you from the turn of the first page."

Of course you know right where I go . . . back into the library to grab Maria.

"Found a friend, Ms. Tremt," I say a few moments later. "Where are we taking the book?"

"You're not taking it anywhere, Kai," Ms. Tremt says. "It's taking you."

"Kai, what's going on here?" Maria says. "We have a lot of work to do on our project. I don't want to get sidetracked."

"Don't worry, Maria," Ms. Tremt says. "You won't lose any time. I promise your adventure will be over in a blink of an eye. In present time, of course."

Ms. Tremt is kind of losing me here. I have no idea what she's talking about.

"Can you explain it like I'm five?" I ask Ms. Tremt.

"Of course," Ms. Tremt says. "I am the keeper of this book. And being the keeper, I also have the honor of sending a few children on time-traveling adventures."

"Figuratively," Maria says.

"No, quite literally," Ms. Tremt says. "I am talking about actual time travel. Let's do a little show-and-tell. Like you're five."

Ms. Tremt pulls a fountain pen out of her

pocket. It's glowing. I start thinking about all the strange things that happened today, like Mr. Tempo and the Mesozoic mammal incident. And now all this. Maybe I didn't get enough sleep last night.

Ms. Tremt opens *The Book of Memories* and uses the sparkling fountain pen to sign her name on the card in it. A question magically appears on the page.

Where would you like to go today?

Maria reaches over, grabs my hand and squeezes it. Cool!

"Let me demonstrate the infinite possibilities that await you," Ms. Tremt says.

She writes *Mexico, February 1519* with the fountain pen. Then she closes the book.

I feel Maria squeeze my hand even tighter as the book begins to shake and grow bigger and bigger, until it appears to take up the whole wall.

"Open the book, Kai," Ms. Tremt says.

I pull open the cover and it's like a movie scene is projected onto the wall.

The scene is set in an ancient city surrounded by snowy mountaintops. There's an enormous pyramid in the center of the city. There's also a warrior standing right in front of us holding a golden shield and wearing a feathered helmet.

Ms. Tremt cautiously puts her hand up toward the scene. It appears inside the image. The warrior holds up the shield defensively. Ms. Tremt taps the shield, which makes a ringing sound, and then pulls her hand back into the room. Then she closes the book, and we all stare as it shrinks back down to normal size.

"What the what?" I gasp.

"I think we should go," Maria says.

"In there?" I ask.

"No, home," Maria says.

"I understand, Maria," Ms. Tremt says. "Time travel is not without its dangers. And there are rules that we will have to review, because the fate of the future will be in your hands."

"Ms. Tremt, is this really an actual thing?" I wonder. "And not a joke?"

"Not a joke," Ms. Tremt says. "An opportunity. A wrinkle in the fabric of time, if you will, that allows a very brief trip into the past."

"How brief?" I ask.

"Three hours," Ms. Tremt says. "Exactly one hundred and eighty minutes to explore any place and date in the past. I understand that you may have a lot of questions. And that you may need some time to decide on your destination."

I'm sure Maria will want more time, but I've always been more of an impulse thinker. I know exactly where and when I want to go.

"Oahu Sugar Company Plantation, 1900," I say. "That's where I want to go. I want to meet my great-great-great-aunt Akemi."

"Have fun," Maria says, letting go of my hand.

"Aw, really," I say. "You don't want to come?"

"Kai, are you crazy?" Maria says. "What if this is some kind of setup?"

"I assure you, Maria, this is not a setup," Ms. Tremt says. "Other Sands Middle School students have successfully journeyed through *The Book of Memories* and have returned safe and sound. I am not able to share their names, and they are not allowed to speak of their adventures, but I assure you that they are all happy that they went along for the ride."

Matt! I think about the way he looked when Mr. Tempo wrote the dates on the board, and I am sure that Matt's been in this room before.

"Akemi wrote all about ocean life," I say. "We could find out what Hawaii was like back then. Think about how awesome that would be."

"I don't know, Kai," Maria says.

I take Maria's hand and squeeze it.

"Come on," I say. "Just think of all the jokes I can tell you in those three hours."

"Okay, that's a deal-breaker." Maria laughs. "Ocean creatures, great. Lame Kai jokes, I'm staying in the present."

I feel Maria's hand relax, though, and can tell she's starting to think about coming.

"So about those rules . . . ," I say to Ms. Tremt.

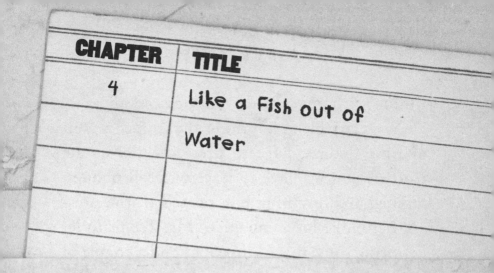

CHAPTER	TITLE
4	Like a Fish out of Water

Maria has a ton of questions about the rules. Every time Ms. Tremt tells us a new rule, Maria has three questions.

I'll give you the summary version, though.

We have three hours. Not a second more. If we don't get the book out and step into the present within the three-hour period, we'll be stuck in the past forever.

So that one really freaked Maria out, but I assured her that I'm a pretty time-sensitive kind of guy, having to think so much about timing with my comedy routines and all.

We can't bring anything that appears "out of time," so we have to dress in appropriate clothes, and we have to leave our cell phones, money, and anything else related to the present behind. Maria convinces Ms. Tremt to let her bring some folded-up paper and a couple of charcoal pencils so she can sketch while she's there.

We have to limit our interactions with people from the past. We can talk to them, but we can't influence their decisions or anything like that. One tiny change in the past could shape the future in big, unknown ways.

And then there are the scarves. Super-stretchy safety nets made of a special nano-fabric that can be scrunched up to the size of a small bouncy ball. In an emergency, we can wrap them around ourselves and they will make us look like nothing is amiss. Maria's eyes get really big just at the mention of the word "emergency."

Miss Tremt also gives us info about Hawaii in 1900.

Hawaii became an annexed territory of the United States in 1898. It did not become a state until 1959.

Sanford B. Dole was governor of Hawaii in 1900.

(Yes, Dole like Dole pineapples. His cousin James Dole founded the company.)

Sugarcane and pineapple plantations became an important industry in the 1890s. Thousands of immigrants arrived from places like China, Japan, the Philippines, and Portugal to work on the plantations.

One pound of sugar cost 7 cents.

The Iolani Palace, once home to the Hawaiian ruling family, had electricity in 1886, before the White House had electric power!

Ms. Tremt pulls out a box of clothes and starts throwing things at us.

"Okay, this outfit is going to have to stay a secret," I tell Maria, putting on a straw hat and sunglasses.

"I'll never tell!" Maria says. "Mine is so much worse!"

I have to agree. I'm wearing a long-sleeve button-down shirt and baggy pants. They're not exactly today's style, especially with the hat, but they could pass. Maria's outfit is straight out of the history files. Straw hat, polka-dotted shirt, and long, baggy skirt.

"Are you sure you don't want to think this through before you go?" Ms. Tremt asks when I tell her that I'm off to the bathroom to change.

"There's no time like the present, right, Maria?" I say.

"Yeah, it's a real gift." She snickers.

"You made a joke!" I cry. "I am totally rubbing off on you."

I grab the clothes and head to the bathroom, making sure none of my friends see me walking down the hall. Improv is not really my thing, and

I don't want to have to make up an excuse on the spot.

I push against the door, but it doesn't open all the way. I shove it a little, and that's when I hear a splashing sound. A janitor is crouched down on the other side of the door, next to a large bucket full of water. Puddles of water are pooled on the floor. I guess I did that.

"Excuse me," I say, and the janitor looks up at me and mumbles.

As I go into the stall to change, I realize that the janitor kind of looks like Mr. Tempo. I only got one quick look at his face, though. But I've definitely never seen this janitor around Sands before.

I get changed quickly and the janitor is already wheeling his bucket down the hallway. That's when I get a look at his hands. He's wearing green gloves! It *is* Mr. Tempo! No way!

I rush back into the library and tell Ms. Tremt about him.

"I have a feeling this isn't the last you'll see of Mr. Tempo. You're going to have to be extra careful on the trip," Ms. Tremt says. "And if you want to back out now, I understand."

"It's okay, Maria," I say. "You don't have to join me. I understand."

Maria shoves me so hard the straw hat falls off my head.

"Shut up, Kai," she says. "I didn't put on this silly outfit just to go home. And I love a good mystery! So who is this guy, anyway?"

Ms. Tremt explains that Mr. Tempo, aka new janitor guy aka substitute math teacher, also known as Tim Raveltere, is a fellow time traveler.

"He's dead set on getting *The Book of Memories,*" Ms. Tremt explains.

"And that's a bad thing?" I ask.

"Very bad," Ms. Tremt says. "If he sees you with the book, he'll try anything to take it from you, and if he gets his hands on it, he's going to use it for nefarious purposes."

"We'd better make sure he doesn't get it," Maria says. "Let's go now."

"Wait a minute," I say to her. "You were totally worried when you thought we were just going to take a nice little trip back into the past. Now you're dying to go when we find out there's actually some real danger involved?"

"Pretty much," Maria says. "You got a problem with that?"

"Not at all." I laugh. "I like the way you think! What are we waiting for?"

Ms. Tremt takes out her fountain pen again, removes the card, and writes *Oahu Sugar Company Plantation, Waipahu, Hawaii,* on the card.

"Did you have a specific date in the year 1900 in mind?" Ms. Tremt asks me.

"Well, according to her diary, Akemi seemed like she was the most homesick right around her birthday," I say. "So maybe November 17, 1900, would be a good day."

"Perfect," Ms. Tremt says as she writes the date on the card.

Once *The Book of Memories* is activated, a scene that looks like it could be on the front of a postcard appears before us. There are long stretches of sugarcane fields and rows of triangle-shaped thatched-roof huts at the plantation.

It's the colors, though, that are incredible. In the scene before us, we see bright green fields and rows and rows of palm trees, and golden sand on the beach. And that's nothing compared to the color of the water. It's dark blue and turquoise, and I just want to jump in it right now.

"Can we?" Maria asks.

"Can we what?" I ask back.

"Can we jump in it first?" she asks.

"Did I say that out loud?" I ask, a little startled.

"You did." Maria and Ms. Tremt laugh.

"Okay, then let's hit the beach first," I say. "And then we'll look for Akemi."

Maria takes my hand again and we step into the book together.

Here's the thing Ms. Tremt forgot to tell me. Once we've completely stepped into the past, the classroom disappears behind us, and suddenly I'm left holding *The Book of Memories*, now pocket-size. Which would be fine, except that before I can even appreciate the view, a hand grabs the book and starts to snatch it from me.

"Mr. Tempo!" Maria shouts.

I look up and see that she's correct. The hand that is holding on to the book is covered in a green glove, and Mr. Tempo—Tim Raveltere, really—is using his watch to activate a whole different kind of portal. All I can see inside the portal is a dark laboratory filled with different time-keeping devices from throughout history, like sundials, hourglasses, and pocket watches.

I don't want to break *The Book of Memories*. (Is that even possible? I don't want to find out.) I'm trying to decide whether to just pull the book as hard as I can and hope for the best when Maria jumps on Tim's back and puts her hands over his eyes.

It's the perfect move, because he automatically reaches up to pull her hands off, and when he does, he lets go of the book. I start running down the beach but then I'm grabbed by Tim, who still has Maria attached to his back. Right next to us a portal appears in the sand. This portal is definitely Tim's doing and not from The Book of Memories. It looks like it might be a gladiator scene from ancient Rome, and I definitely don't want to go there!

Maria pulls Tim's hair, and I roll away from the portal. Then I see another portal pop up next to Maria—is that a Yeti?!?—and Tim's just about to toss her off his back and into it.

"NOOOO!!!" I yell as I run to Maria.

I grab her and try to swing us both over the portal. Sand flies everywhere as I land and trip and roll over into the water. I can't see anything because my eyes are full of sand, but for a second it seems like my move worked. We're definitely not in some different time period, but somehow we've landed in the middle of the ocean. There's no land in sight. So we avoided going through the portal, but I think somehow we brushed up against it and it bounced us out to sea.

"You *wanted* danger?" I gasp.

"Come on, that was pretty awesome," Maria says breathlessly. "Did you see me totally take out Mr. Tempo?"

"You mean Tim the Time Traveling Terror?" I correct her. "Yeah, I caught that."

So I'm treading water, which is difficult to do because Maria is leaning on my shoulder so she can hold *The Book of Memories* over her head. We don't know if it's okay for the book to get wet or not. I do know that it's okay for Maria to be holding on to my shoulder, though. I take one of Ms. Tremt's scarves out of my pocket and, surprisingly, it's bone dry. I wrap the book in it for protection. If the scarves are really as magical as Ms. Tremt claims they are, hopefully it will keep the book safe from danger . . . and water.

"I think we should go that way," Maria says, using the book to point off into the distance to the right of us. "I don't think we went back in time. I didn't get the same feeling as when we walked through the library portal. So I think we just got tossed a little farther by the power of the portal."

"I agree," I tell Maria. "With the whole portal thing. But not with the direction. Because I feel like we rolled left."

"Definitely not, Kai," Maria huffs. "It was a right roll. I'm sure."

"I don't always have to be right," I say. "I'd admit it if I didn't know. But it was left."

"Kai!" Maria yells.

"What?" I yell back.

"What's that sound?" she asks.

"How can I tell when you're yelling?" I laugh.

We both shut up and listen to a sound of rhythmic splashing. Together, we turn slowly around in place. That's when we see them. Far off in the distance, two people are paddling on surfboards. There's hope!

"HEY!" I scream. "OVER HERE!"

"YO!" Maria calls out.

"Yo?" I laugh. "Is that your idea of Hawaiian slang?"

Maria pushes against me and we both start yelling whatever silly thing comes to mind.

"HEY, PLAYERS!" Maria shouts.

"HOLLA!" I roar.

"WHAT'S UP, WHAT'S UP, WHAT'S UP???" Maria yells.

We hope they'll hear us. But if we're left stranded out here, at least we can make each other laugh.

Our bigmouth shouting works, and once the paddlers get closer, we can tell that it's a boy and a girl.

"How did you get all the way out here?" the girl calls to us. "And what do you have wrapped up in that scarf?"

"We were . . . um . . . floating on a raft," Maria stammers.

"Yeah . . . um . . . reading together," I add, trying to help Maria think quickly.

"And then the raft sank." Maria sighs. "So,

here we are. I'm glad you spotted us."

"Your raft sank?" the boy wonders, looking around for signs of it. "I never heard of that happening before."

"I know," I say. "I've got a lot to learn about raft building."

"He really does," Maria agrees.

I splash Maria in response to her comment.

"You know, it would be great to get some help back to the beach," I suggest.

"Of course!" the girl replies. "I'm sorry. I'm Leilani, and this is my brother, Tua. Aloha!"

"Aloha," Maria says. "I'm Maria, and this is Kai. Nice to meet you."

Leilani starts to chuckle.

"Your parents chose the perfect name, Kai," she says. "In Hawaiian, Kai means 'from the sea.' Is your mom's name Nāmaka?"

"Close. It's Tomoko," I say, confused.

Tua helps his sister onto his surfboard.

"She's just teasing you, Kai," he explains. "Nāmaka is the Hawaiian sea goddess."

"Got it," I say. I hold the book while Maria climbs on to Leilani's board, then I give it to her while I climb up behind her. We're a little shaky at first, and it's hard to keep up with Leilani and Tua, who seem to be expert surfers.

"You know, I've always wanted to try surfing," Maria confesses.

"Me too," I agree. "This is great. I could paddle out here all day."

I'm not so worried about how far ahead Leilani and Tua are, because it's kind of like Maria and I are paddling on our own little island. Until I see the fin. That's right—a *fin*!

I know Maria likes danger, but I don't want her to panic. My dad made me watch *Jaws*, so I know the worst thing you can do is start flapping your legs around in the water. It's like turning yourself into shark bait.

I tap Maria and bring my legs carefully up onto the board.

"Legs up," I say calmly to her.

"Is this some kind of surf lesson?" she asks.

"No," I say, pointing to the fin. "Don't panic, but this is because of . . . that."

"A shark!" Maria gasps. "Are you kidding me? Now what do we do?"

We try to stay as still as we can while we wave our arms in the air, hoping Leilani and Tua will see us. Leilani turns around and smiles back at us and shakes her head. Tua points off in the opposite direction. We have no idea what they're trying to tell us, until we turn around and see the huge wave that is heading right for us.

Fin . . . wave . . . wave . . . fin. It's an impossible choice. Maria and I just hang on to each other and close our eyes, and when the wave hits, we're swept off the board and are floating in the water again. So is the fin.

"Not a bad first surfing attempt." Tua laughs as he paddles over to us.

I have no idea why he's laughing, because again . . . *fin*!

Leilani hops off the board and starts to swim toward us.

"Leilani!" I cry. "What are you doing?"

"Look out for the fin!" Maria adds, sounding panicked.

"You two are funny." Leilani giggles. "You're scared of a dolphin?"

Leilani swims right toward the fin and pats

it. A dolphin raises its head up above the surface of the water, like it's saying hello to an old friend, then dives back down and disappears.

"Yeah, dolphin, I knew that," I bluff.

We get back on our boards and paddle to land. After we finally crawl onto the sand, Maria and I just lie on the beach panting. Paddling is hard work! Then I remember *The Book of Memories*. I panic and frantically look around until Maria taps my shoulder and holds it up. "It's perfectly fine," she says. That scarf really did the trick.

I check out the book. It's completely dry, as is the scarf, even though they were both just in the ocean. Pretty cool. And amazing.

"You two could really use a surfing lesson," Tua says. "We would have been back to the beach a lot faster!"

"Only if it's a quick one," I say. "We've got to meet my aunt—I mean my cousin—in a little while."

Maria and I get on the boards and Tua demonstrates in the sand. Of course the lesson starts with more paddling, which is pretty much the last thing I feel like doing right now. He shows us how to push up from paddling position, flat on your stomach on the board, to surf stance.

"Don't get on your knees," Tua tells me. "It looks easier, but you'll start too slow then."

"Okay," I say.

It's not so hard, on the sand.

"And don't spread your legs too far," Leilani says. "It might feel better, but you'll have more control with your feet closer together."

Maria and I practice pushing up from the boards a few times.

"I'm ready," I say. "Let's try it out."

"Sure you are." Tua laughs.

He takes us out one at a time. We walk out into the water until we're waist deep. Tua points to a spot where the waves are breaking and tells me to paddle out there.

I sit on the board and wait for the right wave. When I see one, I paddle over to catch it and then push up on my board.

I get to stand for exactly two seconds on the board, and then I'm flailing around in the water again.

When it's Maria's turn, she makes it a full five seconds before she falls off.

"Show-off!" I call to her when she gets back to the beach.

"Just admit I'm better all around." Maria laughs.

"Okay, you're better," I agree. "But not all around. I'm still the king of comedy."

"I'll give you that." Maria laughs. "But we'd better get going. Three hours, right?"

Leilani knows exactly where the Oahu Sugar Company Plantation is, and luckily it's just down the road from the beach, so we don't have to waste a lot of time getting there. We say "aloha" to the Leilani and Tua—it means "good-bye," too—and head down the road.

We meet some workers along the way and I ask them if they know Akemi Takahashi. It takes a few minutes, but we find Akemi's home and I can hardly believe my eyes.

I knew, from reading her journal, that Akemi was really sad. Homesick and all alone, working long and hard every day. I just had no idea how tough her life was too. Even though she wrote about her life and described her home in detail, I still didn't picture it like this. I'm a kid who lives in a nice house, with a room of my own that is way bigger than this little hut. I have a big, comfy bed, my own computer, pretty much all the sports equipment I'll ever need.

Akemi has almost nothing. There's a flat mat on the floor and a wooden chair and a small, low table on one side of the room. Her journal is sitting on the table. There's a small trunk on the other side of the room. And that's it. It's dark and colorless. It feels like a different world from the beautiful place right outside the door.

"No wonder she writes so much about the outside world," Maria says. "I'd want to forget my life in here too. So depressing."

We head back out into the field and start to check out the plantation. Luckily it's hot enough that our clothes dry out a bit, and since all the workers are drenched with sweat anyway, we look like we fit right in. Maria and I find some hoes near a shed, and we pick them up and pretend to be digging the ground as we go.

We ask about Akemi as we work, and it doesn't

take too long for us to find her. She's shy, and a hard worker, keeping her eyes to the ground the whole time. Maria and I work our way around so that we're digging on either side of her.

"*Konnichiwa*," I say to Akemi as I hold my hoe to the side and bow.

She glances up at me and bows her head.

This is going to be tough. It will probably just be easier to talk to Maria so Akemi can see how friendly we are.

"Hey, Maria," I say. "What did the pineapple tree say to the farmer?"

"I don't know, Kai, what?" Maria says.

"Stop picking on me!" I joke.

Maria starts to giggle. Akemi just keeps digging.

"Why shouldn't you tell secrets on a farm?"

"Why?" Maria asks.

"Because the potatoes have eyes and the corn has ears."

Maria groans. Akemi keeps on digging.

"Knock-knock," Maria says.

"Who's there?" I ask.

"Farmer," Maria replies.

"Famer who?"

"Farmer birthday, I would like a nice big cake." Maria giggles.

I groan. Akemi starts to giggle. Progress!

Maria is pretty good at making up jokes. This one was just as corny as the ones I made up. Maybe I could hire her to write jokes for me? Something else for me to think about.

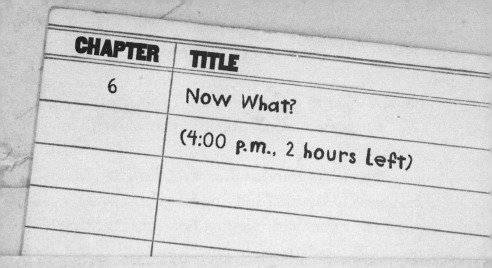

Maria and I don't want to scare off Akemi, so we work quietly next to her for a while.

"How long have you been here?" Maria asks.

"Eight months," Akemi says. "I arrived last March."

"Do you think you'll stay long?" I ask.

Of course, I know the answer. Akemi will never go back to Japan. She'll get married and stay in Hawaii for the rest of her life.

"Possibly another year or two," she says. "I'm sending almost all my money to my family back home. When they have enough, I will return."

"What about you?" Akemi asks Maria. "Do you have family?"

Maria looks at me as if to say, *Great, what am I supposed to say now?* Judging from her answer, I guess she agrees with me that honesty is the best policy. Without giving too much away, of course.

"I live with my mom and dad and my two older brothers," Maria says.

"And you?" Akemi asks me.

"Same," I say. "Except for the big brothers. I have a big sister."

"Yumi's awesome," Maria says out of the blue.

"Why would you say that?" I ask.

"She always looks so well put-together, and she's so talented," Maria says. "I've always looked up to her. Even though we don't really know each other."

"Really?" I say, surprised. "I had no idea. I have a pretty great family," I admit to Akemi. "My sister is really talented, and my dad teaches me a lot, and my mom is the funniest person I know."

"You'll like my family, too, Kai," Maria says.

76

"My dad is a big prankster. And of course my brothers have followed in his footsteps."

"I've heard the rumors." I laugh. "They're the ones who glued fake spiders to the bathroom ceiling at Sands, right?"

"That's them." Maria laughs.

Akemi doesn't seem to be paying attention to us anymore. She's looking down at the ground again, and I see a few wet drops hit the dirt where she's standing.

"Is it starting to rain?" I wonder, looking up at the sky.

"No, Kai," Maria says. "Pay attention!"

Maria points to Akemi. She's still looking down, but now her shoulders are shaking a little. She's crying!

"This isn't good, Kai," Maria whispers. "We're supposed to be cheering her up."

She goes over and puts her arm around Akemi.

"Are you okay?" Maria asks.

"I'm not!" Akemi sobs. "I miss my mom and dad. I miss my brother and sisters. I miss my home. I don't have any friends here. I'm so tired. I'm so sad."

Maria hugs her a little tighter.

Akemi wipes her eyes.

"Maybe we should talk about something else," Maria suggests. "My mom always says that when you need a cry, just let it out, but don't dwell in it."

"Akemi," I say. "Do you know why oysters never share their pearls?"

Akemi doesn't answer. She just shakes her head.

"It's because they're shellfish," I say.

"Kai is getting ready to perform for a comedy contest," Maria explains to Akemi. "In case you were wondering why he's obsessed with bad jokes."

"Hey, they're not all bad," I protest. I turn back to Akemi and ask, "How does the ocean greet a surfer?"

Akemi looks up at me, smiles, brushes a tear off her cheek, and whispers, "It waves."

I can see a tiny ray of hope, but I don't want to push the jokes too much. Then, all of a sudden, my stomach starts to growl like a trapped tiger.

Akemi giggles. "We can get some food now," she says.

Maria and I follow Akemi through the fields until we reach a building with large open doors. Tables are stretched from one end to the other, and workers are lining up to get their meals. Others are sitting down at the tables and quickly gobbling up their food.

We follow Akemi in line and I get a tray. First on my plate, a heap of rice. Of course. Then I get a heaping of tofu stew. I can see their vegetable garden out the window. There are plantation workers outside tending to their gardens. The daikon radishes, eggplants, and string beans that are in my stew have come straight from that garden.

There is a lot more going on in the dining room than there was in Akemi's room, but it is just as dismal. All the workers are dirty, sweaty, and look exhausted. There's not a lot of conversation because most of the workers have just enough energy left to scoop the food into their mouths. Akemi, though, is a lot chattier than she was before. She's asking Maria questions about her family, her home, and the things she likes to do. When Akemi looks away for a moment, Maria gives me the thumbs-up sign.

After we finish eating, we walk back with Akemi. She seems so much happier than she did just a little while ago.

But apparently not happy enough. As soon as Akemi gets into her room, she drags the trunk over and starts to put her few belongings inside it.

"Wh-wh-what are you doing?" I blurt out.

"This isn't the place for me," Akemi tells us. "You've convinced me of that. I miss my family too much. You reminded me what is really important in life. I need to be home, in Japan, with my family."

Maria and I look at each other in horror. We've *totally* messed this trip up!

"Hold on, Akemi," I say. "We'll be right back."

Maria and I head out for a quick team conference, but when I pass Akemi's trunk, I see the strangest thing. There's the glimmer of green in the small pile of Akemi's clothes, and it looks exactly like the shade of green of Tim Raveltere's gloves.

"This is an epic *disaster*!" I moan to Maria when we get outside.

"Suck it up, Kai," Maria says. "Maybe Akemi *should* go home. Maybe she needs to be with her family. You saw how sad she was."

"NOOOO!" I cry. "If Akemi goes home, my family will never move to Hawaii. And never mind the consequences of . . . Hello? No Hawaii, no Kai. It will mean that my grandmother won't exist either, and she was one of the first marine biologists to fight for the protection of endangered fish here. If she's never born, she'll never get to do all her important work. The future of Hawaii's wildlife is at risk, Maria! Don't you even care about that?"

"CARE?" Maria yells back at me. "Of course I care. I just didn't think of that. What are we waiting for? We need to figure out a better plan—*now*!"

I look around and see the path we first walked up to get to Akemi's.

"The beach," I remind Maria. "Akemi loves it there. She writes about the ocean and the wildlife here all the time in her journal."

"So do you think it's time to ask Akemi for a tour?" Maria asks.

"It is," I say.

I am pretty sure our plan is going to work, but when we go back inside, Akemi is gone. And since there's really nowhere for her to be hiding in here, we have no idea where she could be. Did Tim Raveltere get her? Did she disappear through some time portal? We search for clues and then we find some out back—a trail of muddy footprints leading off in the opposite direction of the beach path.

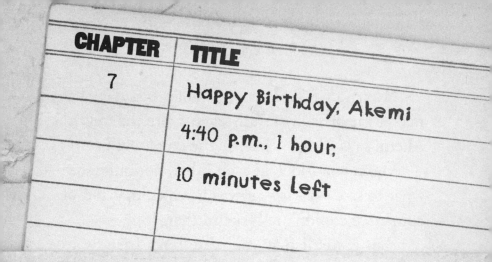

The path actually swirls around and leads to a different spot along the water's edge. It's a quiet, shady area surrounded by palm trees, like a little secret nature room. Rocky ledges surround a pool of blue-green water, and Akemi is sitting on one of the biggest rocks, wiping away tears.

"I'm sorry, Kai. I'm sorry, Maria," she says when she sees us. "I'm not very good company today. It's just that . . . today is a difficult day for me, and I feel sad."

"Did they give you more work?" Maria asks.

"No, no," Akemi says. "Today is a day that makes me miss my family even more than ever," Akemi says. "It's . . . it's . . . the day I was born."

Maria and I look at each other, not quite sure what to say. We knew it was her birthday, but of course we couldn't tell Akemi that.

"I'm grateful that you were both friendly to me," Akemi adds. "And it was really nice to meet you. I really enjoyed spending time with you."

"Happy birthday, Akemi," I say quietly, and Maria repeats it.

I get a feeling that this spot is a sacred place to Akemi, and that any joking, or trying make a bigger deal of Akemi's birthday, is not the right move. We don't have any wiggle room—if I make the wrong move now, I might never exist in the present! So Maria and I find rocks near Akemi and sit on them silently. Maria takes out her paper and pencils and starts to sketch.

As I look around, I realize that I know this spot, actually. I've read about it in Akemi's journal. We sit together, and I start to see that it's not just beautiful because of the trees and sweet-smelling flowers. There's an incredible, busy world of wildlife around us. Brightly colored birds call to one another in the trees. A blue butterfly lands on a nearby flower.

"This is a magical spot," Maria whispers as she draws. "It feels like it was sprinkled with fairy dust."

"Totally," I say.

"It's my favorite place on the island," Akemi admits. "I love to just sit here and watch."

"I can see why," I tell her.

"Can you show us more, Akemi?" Maria asks. "I'd love to see the island that you see."

Akemi leads us through the trees and points out all the wildlife around us. I know from her journal that she'll never go to high school, and she hasn't studied biology, but she's a natural. She knows exactly where to find the most amazing things. Like if we look inside the flower of the pitcher plant, we'll find a pool of water, or if we turn over a rock, there's a skink (a tiny lizard) living underneath.

"You really love nature," Maria observes. "I do too."

"It's why I wanted to come here," Akemi

admits. "Of course, my first thought is for my family. I have to work so I can send money back home and help out. But I imagined that I would do so much more than just work here."

"Then why don't you?" I ask.

"Why don't I what?" Akemi wonders.

"Why don't you stay," I say to her, "and do so much more than just work here?"

Akemi puts her head down and closes her eyes. She takes a deep breath. I take one too, and it smells like the ocean breeze mixed with the sweet smell of plumeria blossoms. Akemi doesn't answer me, but I know I've given her something to think about.

We quietly follow the trail as it loops around. Maria spots a bird sitting in a giant, star-shaped flower. She takes out her paper and pencil again and sketches it. Akemi points to a pink flower with curled, waxy petals.

"Pink torch ginger," she tells Maria.

Maria starts to sketch the flowers. That's when we begin to hear the shouts.

"STOP!" A girl's voice echoes through the trees.

"That sounds like Leilani!" Maria says.

"PUT THAT DOWN!" a boy yells.

"And Tua!" I say.

We race down the path to find out what's going on.

Tim Raveltere is what's going on, or more specifically, Tua is holding our sneaky former substitute teacher in a wrestling grip. He's wearing only one green glove, though.

"I knew that was one of his gloves in Akemi's trunk," I whisper to Maria.

I'm afraid that if Tua lets go of his arms, Tim will activate his time-travel watch and make a portal appear. I'm not quite sure how I'll explain that to Akemi, Leilani, and Tua, so I walk over to help Tua out, when Akemi storms past me.

"He was trying to take these!" Leilani says to Akemi, pointing to a pile of eggs wrapped up in a scarf.

Tim tries to talk his way out of it.

"Come on, guys," he says. "I was hungry. I haven't eaten in years—I mean hours—and they looked good."

"They looked good?!?" Akemi huffs. "Do you know what kind of eggs those are?!"

"Those are honu eggs," Tua growls into Tim's ear. "Don't *ever* touch them."

I'm not really sure what a honu is, but I'm guessing they're pretty important around here. Leilani can see the confusion on my face.

"Honu is our green sea turtle," she explains. "For all Hawaiians, it is a good-luck symbol, our guardian spirit."

"Honu stands for the link between man, the land, and the sea," Tua adds. "Our stories tell of a special honu, named Kauila, who would turn into a human girl and protect the children playing on the beach. When Kauila's mother dug her nest, a spring of water spouted from the ground, giving the children water to drink."

"Those turtles have been part of the islands, part of our world, for a lot longer than we have," Akemi adds. "Like Tua said—*don't ever touch them*!"

Leilani explains that we will have to get the turtle eggs back to their nest and buried as soon as possible so they can hatch when they are ready.

Tua and Maria agree to stay with Tim while we search the beach to find the place where Tim dug up the eggs.

Suddenly I see Maria tug on Tim's ear. Hard.

"Listen, Mr. Tempo," she snarls. "No tricky time stuff. I'm in no mood!"

Ha! And my friend Faris thinks Maria is quiet!

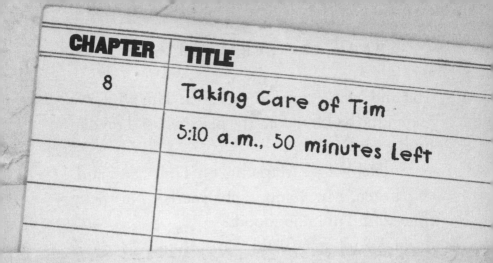

CHAPTER	TITLE
8	Taking Care of Tim
	5:10 a.m., 50 minutes left

Akemi zigs and zags up and down the beach, intent on finding the right spot for the eggs.

"Cup the eggs in your hands," she tells me and Leilani. "It will keep them warm and incubating."

"You got it," I say.

"And walk slowly and steadily," Akemi adds. "It's important not to jostle them!"

I walk as if I am holding my mom's favorite Satsuma vases. I would be grounded in my room for a year if I ever did anything to "jostle" them.

I hear a splashing sound and look out to see an enormous fin poke out of the water.

"Watch!" Akemi tells me.

A giant gray body emerges on the surface as a humpback whale leaps above the water, then dives back down again.

"That's off the hook!" I shout. "I can't believe I just saw that."

"Oh no, there are no hooks involved," Akemi corrects me. "No one is catching that whale. It is breaching."

"Right." I chuckle.

I mean, I can't explain "off the hook" without revealing something about the time period I come from, so I'm just going to have to let Akemi think I'm some kind of whale newbie.

"There are ships that hunt them, though," Akemi says sadly. "I don't know why they'd want to take those gentle giants from the world."

Akemi points to the waters closer to the shore, and I can see a dense school of striped fish swim right by us. Then she taps my shoulder and points back toward the trees. A Hawaiian goose, the nene, waddles through the trees with three goslings close behind her. I wish Maria were here to sketch all this.

Akemi keeps on looking in the sand for the right spot. Her love of all things natural is transformative. Her face looks so different right now than it did when we first saw her working in the field. She looks bright and beautiful. And she's so inspired by the nature around her. I have to admit, I am too.

Finally, Akemi finds the spot.

"I've got this," I say, but then I trip on a waterlogged branch and nearly drop the eggs.

Akemi quickly scoops the eggs from me and places them down in the sand. Leilani places hers, and then we cover them up. We wait and watch for a few minutes until we're sure that no one is going to disturb them.

"Aloha, honu keiki," Leilani whispers to the eggs. "Safe travels to the ocean."

When we get back, I realize that we may have made a mistake leaving "tough guys" Tua and Maria in charge of Tim. They've tied him up to Tua's surfboard and are pushing him out to sea.

"Wait!" I yell, feeling conflicted. "I mean, I don't think he's a good guy, but I'm not sure that he's a *bad* guy either. We don't want to put him in danger or anything. That wouldn't be right. You know, right to a fair trial and all that."

Maria pinches Tim's ankle and he yelps.

"See if you feel the same way after you hear this, Kai," she says.

Tua asks about the book that Maria was holding when they first found us floating out in the ocean.

"Is it yours?" he says.

"Not technically," I admit. "A friend loaned it to me."

"I told you it's mine!" Tim yells. "I'm the friend."

"You are *sooo* not my friend," I protest. "And the book is not yours. Be real."

"Okay, okay," Tim says. "Like I told you before, it's not exactly mine, but the 'friend' who gave it to him, Ms. Tremt, is a witch. An evil witch who has plans to ignite every volcano on the islands until they melt into the sea."

"You're a joke." I laugh. "Tua, that is totally untrue."

"Told ya," Maria says triumphantly to Tua.

"I already believed you." Tua laughs. He turns back to Tim. "No book for you!"

"What about my glove, then?" Tim moans. "At least let me get my glove back!"

"You and that glove!" Maria says as she pinches him again. "I already told you how you're going to get it back." I don't know why Tim wants his glove back so badly, but I figure his gloves must contain some sort of magical power or he would just let it go.

Maria explains that she realized Tim was probably searching through Akemi's hut looking for us (or signs of the book) when he dropped the glove. She and Tua agreed that the perfect way to ensure Tim doesn't make any more trouble for us is to send him off on an "adventure" mission.

"First he'll have to figure out how to untangle the vine so he can get his arms and legs free," Tua explains. "Don't worry, Kai. They're pretty loose. There's no real danger."

"Then he'll have to surf—or swim—back to shore?" Leilani guesses.

"Exactly," Tua confirms.

"In the meanwhile, we'll hide his green glove in the sugar-plantation crops," Maria finishes. "It should take him a *long* time to find it in all that greenery!"

"You're brilliant!" I say as I grab Maria and give her a hug.

Maria hugs me back! It's totally awesome.

I hear coughing behind me and I see Tua and Leilani smiling at me.

"It's not like that," I protest.

"Sure it's not," Tua teases.

We all agree that Maria and Tua's plan is golden. We crouch down to push Tim out to sea.

"Please, reconsider this," Tim pleads. "I lied. Valerie Tremt isn't a witch. She's an extraterrestrial being who is gathering information to take back to her home planet. They will invade our planet and destroy all humans on Earth."

"What is he even talking about?" Leilani laughs.

"Nonsense," Maria says, pinching him again. "Didn't I tell you to keep quiet?"

Once Tim is safely out to sea, we race back to Akemi's hut and grab the glove. We weave through the fields, looking for the perfect place to put it.

"Over here!" Leilani calls, standing in the middle of tall sugarcanes.

"No," Akemi says. "We'll probably cut those down tomorrow. The glove will be easy to see then."

"What about here?" Maria asks, pointing to a pile of cane that's been cut.

"Nope," Akemi says. "We can do better."

"I know!" I say. "Follow me!"

I lead the group back to the dining hall and head out back. I find a thick patch of daikon plants full of large green leaves.

"Here?" I ask.

"Perfect!" Akemi cheers.

We place the glove underneath one of the largest leaves, then walk away. It's impossible to see it from a distance. Tim is going to be playing this game of hide-and-seek for a long, long time. But we know his gloves probably contain some kind of magic, so he'll search until he finds it.

The sun is beginning to set, and I know we're going to have to head back home soon. Leilani and Tua have to leave too.

"You should all come over to our house on Saturday," Tua says to us.

"For the *aha'aina*," Leilani says. "It's a special family gathering."

I look over at Maria, who is glaring at me. "Three hours," she hisses.

"I know. I know," I say to her.

"It does sounds like fun . . . ," Akemi says tentatively.

"It does," Maria agrees. "But Kai and I have something to do on Saturday."

"Oh, too bad." Akemi sighs. "Then I probably won't be around either. I'm thinking of going home as soon as I can find a way back."

"Really?" Leilani says. "That's too bad. I was hoping we could check back on the turtle eggs together. You know, make sure they stay safe and protected from predators like Tim."

"You were?" Akemi says, surprised. "I think I'd like that."

"I could show you some of my other favorite spots on the island," Leilani says. "Since I grew up here, I know them all."

"Do you know where I could see a red-footed

booby?" Akemi asks hopefully.

"A sula sula?" Tua says. "I know where you can find them!"

"I've been dying to see one up close!" Akemi says. Her face is shining with excitement.

"We'll stop by to see if you decide to stay, then," Tua says.

"I hope you do," Leilani adds.

"And if your plans change, come to our house on Saturday," Tua tells us. "Just keep following the path away from the beach until you get to the village. You'll hear us!"

We all wave good-bye to the brother and sister. I think about how lucky we were to meet them.

"I really like them," Akemi admits.

"I do too," I say. "They seem like they would be good friends."

"Since you mentioned friends, I was wondering if you have time to stop by before you leave," Akemi asks.

I look at Maria again. She isn't glaring.

"As long as it's quick. We really need to leave soon, unfortunately," Maria says.

"Of course. Let's go," Akemi says.

As we walk, Maria remembers something.

"Akemi," she says. "I know someone like you, someone who loves wildlife and the ocean."

"Oh, does he live on the island too?" Akemi asks.

"No, he does not," Maria replies. "He's French, and his nickname is Jeek. But I once read something he wrote that I think you might find interesting."

"Really?" Akemi says. "What is it?"

Maria closes her eyes and thinks for a moment.

"Sometimes we are lucky enough to know that our lives have been changed," she says. "To discard the old, embrace the new, and run head-long down an immutable course."

Akemi closes her eyes and sighs deeply.

"That's beautiful. Can you say that again?" she asks.

Maria does.

When we get back to Akemi's, she dives into her trunk and digs through her things.

"For you," she says, holding out a seashell necklace to Maria.

"It's beautiful!" Maria says. "I love it."

"I'm glad," Akemi says. "I made it myself."

"And for you, Kai, ocean boy," Akemi says.

Akemi gives me a sketch she made of her secret pool. She's not as good an artist as Maria, but the picture is filled with love and she's spent time on every detail.

"I can't take it," I say. "It's your special place."

"It's our special place now," Akemi says. "And you're Japanese! You know it is rude to refuse a gift. What are you thinking?"

What *am* I thinking? I bow deeply and thank Akemi for the sketch.

Maria holds out her empty hands.

"I wish I had something for you," she says. "For your birthday."

"Me too," I add.

"You've already given me something," Akemi tells us.

"We did?" I wonder. "Was it the oyster joke?"

"It was not." Akemi laughs.

"How about this one, then?" I say. "What is the best day to go to the beach?"

"I don't know," Akemi says.

"*Sun*day!" I reply.

Maria and Akemi groan.

"It is definitely not your jokes," Akemi says. "You and Maria have given me something much more special. You have helped me see things in a different light."

"I hope you'll think about staying on the

101

island," I say. "I think they need you here."

"I don't know," Akemi says. "There are already lots of people here, and more coming every week."

"That's why you're so important," Maria says. "Because you're one of the few who cares about the creatures who live on the island who aren't people."

I can tell Akemi's still not totally convinced, but she's also not packing her things.

"Maybe I'll see you at work tomorrow," Akemi says hopefully.

"Probably not," I say. "I . . . I heard they might be moving us to another island for some big job. Pineapples, I think."

"Oh, that's too bad." Akemi sighs. "Good luck, then. I hope we meet again someday."

"I do too," Maria says. "And don't forget: Sometimes we are lucky enough to know that our lives have been changed, to discard the old, embrace the new, and run headlong down an immutable course."

"I won't!" Akemi assures her.

Maria is starting to glare at me again, so we

say our last good-byes and head outside to find a spot to place *The Book of Memories* and time travel back home.

"Let's go to the secret pool," I suggest. "There's probably no one there."

We race down the path, knowing that time is running short. But we have to stop for a second because the view of the ocean is incredible. Tim Raveltere is out in the distance, riding a wave on the surfboard, flailing his arms wildly but still "hanging ten."

"Pretty impressive." I laugh. "I didn't think he had it in him."

"Yeah, we may have to travel back and get some surfing lessons from him." Maria chuckles.

When we get to the pool, we climb on the rocks and find the perfect spot. I take the book out of my pocket and peel the scarf off it.

I open the book, take out the card, and write our home coordinates and time information. I place the card back in and close the book cover. The book trembles and grows right before us. Then Maria opens it again and we see the library at good old Sands Middle School waiting for us.

We wave good-bye to the secret pool, then hold hands and step back home.

"Timely greetings," Ms. Tremt says, looking at her watch. "You two like to live on the edge, I see."

"I told you we were cutting it too close," Maria complains.

"So how was your journey?" Ms. Tremt asks. "Was it everything you expected?"

"More!" I say. "I've been to Hawaii a lot of times to visit my family, but it looked so different in 1900. There weren't any huge hotels or roads with traffic flying by. It's just nature, beautiful and all around you."

"And your great-great-aunt Akemi?" Ms. Tremt says. "She's doing well?"

"She wasn't," I admit. "But I think we helped cheer her up."

"I'm sure you did," Ms. Tremt says seriously. "In fact, I know that you did."

Maria starts to fill Ms. Tremt in on the whole Tim Raveltere craziness, and Ms. Tremt doesn't seem surprised at all.

"He's a nuisance," Ms. Tremt says. "And I'm

glad he'll be out of the time-travel picture for a while. You are a master scheme-maker, Maria."

"You should see her wrestling moves!" I laugh.

"Oh, I did," Ms. Tremt says.

Maria and I look at Ms. Tremt, confused.

"I mean, I'm sure," Ms. Tremt says quickly. "How would I have seen them?"

Ms. Tremt offers to stay late in the library so we can work more on our Be the Change project, but we're both exhausted.

"I think I need to go home to a long shower," I say. "I'm not used to plowing the fields and stuff."

"Same here," Maria says. "But we'll be back at the library tomorrow."

I feel like collapsing the second I get home, but I will remind you that I was doing hard labor all day, so that long bath, it's definitely needed.

"Phewie," Mom says, waving the air around me. "That must have been some tough workout."

"MOM!" I complain.

"If your mother can't tell you that you stink, who can?" Mom laughs.

"True." I laugh too. "I'm so smelly, the judge said, "Odor in the court.""

"Good one," Mom says. "Don't forget to write it down."

After I'm all cleaned up, I plop down on my bed. I should just fall asleep, but I see Akemi's journals calling to me. I pick them up and start to reread them. It all seems a lot different now that I actually know her.

Wait a minute That's when it hits me—I'm here, and Akemi's journals are here too! That must mean that she decided to stay in Hawaii. Which is a huge relief!

Mom taps on my door.

"I know you must be tired, but I just wanted to check to see if you wanted to go over your stand-up routine before you go to sleep," she says. "Seeing as the contest is this Saturday night."

"Saturday!" I say. "Right! I must have lost track of time or something.

I'm really excited for the contest, but I can't help thinking about how much fun it would have been to join the family celebration with Tua and Leilani.

"Do you have something else to do?" Mom asks me.

"Kind of, but it's not going to happen anyway," I tell her.

"That's good," Mom says. "Because I'm not going to let you miss this contest. I know you're going to win!"

"That's what your mom is supposed to say." I laugh. "I'm sure all the other comedians' moms are saying the same thing."

"True," Mom says. "But their moms aren't your mom. Remember, you have the funniest mom around."

Mom contorts her eyes and mouth into a silly monster face. It always cracks me up.

"You're right," I say. "There's no one like you."

I take out my notes and run through some "Did you ever wonder?" lines with Mom. She helps me reword some of them and cross out a few that aren't working.

The thing is, the only "Did you ever wonder?" I want to think about right now is "Did you ever wonder what it's like to live in Hawaii?"

I tell my mom that.

"Are you missing Baba?" she asks.

"I am," I say.

"Me too," Mom admits.

"Can you tell me some of your stories about growing up in Hawaii?" I ask.

"It's been a long time since you asked for a bedtime story, Kai-chan," Mom says.

"I know," I say. "But I'm really in the mood for Hee-Haw the Donkey Man."

"Oh, that's a good one." Mom laughs. "So when I was little, there was a neighbor whose laugh sounded like a donkey braying. All the kids called him Hee-Haw. One day, your uncle Kenji and I were playing baseball outside when . . ."

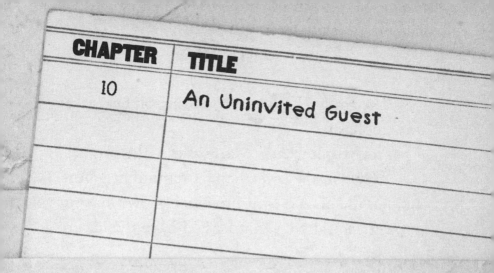

CHAPTER	TITLE
10	An Uninvited Guest

That night I dreamed I went back to Hawaii. I was riding on a surfboard, but it wasn't really a surfboard. It was more like a hoverboard/magic carpet. It floated over the waves and then rose up into the air. Whales and dolphins and rays jumped out of the water to greet me. They followed me like I was the leader of an ocean parade, and as we circled the island, the crowd of creatures grew and grew.

Once I rubbed the sleep out of my eyes, I couldn't wait to see Maria, so as soon as I got to school, I ran to her locker.

"I've got it!" I tell her, pounding on her locker for emphasis.

"You've got what?" Maria asks. "The plague?"

"Hey, I'm the comedian," I remind her. "And no, not the plague. Our project. I know what our project should be. Or at least, I have the idea of a project."

"What is it?" Maria asks.

"I'll tell you in the library," I say. "Come on."

I take her hand and pull her to the library. I can see some kids' eyebrows raise. Gossip flies fast around the halls of Sands Middle School, but we have much more important things to worry about.

We get to the library and it's open, but Ms. Tremt is nowhere to be seen. We do hear some crashing sounds coming from the secret room.

"Ms. Tremt?" I call.

"I hope Tim hasn't found his glove!" Maria gasps.

We head to the room to investigate. Ms. Tremt is crawling around on the floor.

"Hey, Ms. Tremt! Is this a new form of librarian exercise?" I ask, laughing.

Ms. Tremt jumps. Well, as much as you can

jump when you're on the floor on all fours.

"Kai! You startled me," Ms. Tremt says.

"I noticed," I reply. "What's going on?"

"That is going on!" Ms. Tremt says.

She points to the floor, where there is a small spotted bird frozen against the floor tile.

"Oh no!" Maria gasps. "Did it come back with us?"

"Apparently," Ms. Tremt replies.

Ms. Tremt crawls slowly toward it, and just as she's about to get her hands on it, it scurries away. Maria and I try to make a barrier for her, but every time Ms. Tremt gets close, it's a game of Catch that Pigeon. Except not a pigeon, exactly.

Maria and I get on our hands and knees and start crawling around too. The bird is a lot quicker than it looks and keeps rushing between all of our hands and feet. I finally think I'm close enough to get it when it races past us and into the library.

We should have trapped the bird in the small space, because now the task seems nearly impossible. Crawl, snatch, hop. Tiptoe, grab, run. We're rushing all around the room, grasping at the air, and I hope no one opens the door, because if it gets out of here, we're doomed! We can't have a bird from 1900 Hawaii flying around Sands Middle School. It will bring up too many unexplainable questions.

It turns out, we're doomed anyway, because just when Maria is about to get her fingers around the bird, it squeezes into an air vent.

"Maybe it will just find its way outside?" Maria asks hopefully.

"That would be a problem," Ms. Tremt says. "Considering it shouldn't be here at all."

"Why not?" I wonder.

"This elusive bird, this Hawaiian rail, could be a danger to the whole time continuum," Ms. Tremt informs us. "We have to get it back to 1900. You see, this bird is an extinct species. From Hawaii. If it anyone sees it here, in this place, at this time, the results could be disastrous."

That is the best news I've heard all morning!

"Sounds like a job for Team Time Travel Hawaii," I say. "We could bring it back for you!"

"We?" Maria snickers.

"Well, I . . . I . . . uh . . . figured you'd want to . . . ," I stammer.

"You figured, huh?" Maria laughs. "It doesn't matter, because we're not going anywhere if we don't get that bird."

"Let me worry about that," Ms. Tremt says. "Just plan to be ready when I need you."

"Of course!" I say.

"As long as it's not Saturday," Maria adds.

"Why not?" I wonder. "If it's Saturday, we can check in on Akemi and make sure that she goes to Leilani and Tua's family celebration."

"And you'll miss your comedy contest," Maria says pointedly.

"Oh yeah, that thing," I say, trying to downplay it. "Well, it's not really that big of a deal. I can enter another contest anytime."

"Not that big of a deal?" Maria gasps. "Who are you kidding?"

Ms. Tremt starts tapping her desk to interrupt us.

"May I remind you two that I am a master of time travel?" she says. "I don't know when I'll be able to retrieve that bird, but even if it's not until Saturday, there is no reason Kai can't go to Hawaii *and* make the contest." She holds up

The Book of Memories. "And anyway, why are you worrying about time when this book can bring you to whatever time you want?"

Maria and I both look at each other and laugh and feel a little foolish.

"She's right," I say. "Why are we worrying about time? We have a time machine, duh!"

Suddenly, Maria looks like a lightbulb has gone off over her head. She tells us she'll be right back and rushes out of the library.

Alone with Ms. Tremt, I grab my knapsack and pull out a book. It's called *Our Ocean, Our World*. Have you heard about it? It's a family favorite. My grandmother wrote it, and it's all about her experiences as a marine biologist and what she learned about the ways human activity affected the ocean and the creatures in it.

"So you finally read the book I've been hoping you'd read." Ms. Tremt smiles.

"I'm not finished yet," I tell her. "But it's really good. I can't wait to go to Hawaii and talk to Baba about it." I add, "Present-day Hawaii."

"Of course," Ms. Tremt says. "And I share your admiration for this tome. I've read it six times!"

Maria races back into the library, holding a small wire cage in her hands.

"I had to bargain with Ms. Guarino, our science teacher," she tells Ms. Tremt. "She didn't want to give up the cage, so I told her you'd lend her a stack of bio-related books for her class. Just in case you do wrangle up the bird, you're going to need a place to put it."

"I would have given her those books anyway," Ms. Tremt says. "That's what libraries are for!"

"I know," Maria says. "But it helped seal the deal."

"As long as it works," I say. "Just don't give her this book."

I show Maria the book my grandmother wrote.

"*Our Ocean, Our World*," Maria says. "Nice."

"You need to read it next," I tell her. "It gave me the idea for our project."

"Which is?" Maria asks.

"The History of Our Water World!" I cheer.

"What's that?" Maria asks.

"Think about it. We want to teach kids about the ocean and why the wildlife that lives in it is so important to our planet," I say. "But we need to do something memorable, too, so that people will stay involved. Remember what Jeek said about showing people a world they've never seen?"

"I remember," Maria says. "Keep going."

"We have to make it real to them. I can translate some of Akemi's journal, and we can use your sketches to illustrate them. Show them what it was like before our oceans became polluted."

"What Maria *imagined* it was like before," Ms. Tremt corrects me.

"Of course." I laugh. "Based on reading Akemi's words."

"I like it so far," Maria says. "We can turn it into a section on the school website, and maybe publish them too."

"Exactly!" I say. "And I can also get Baba, my grandma, to send me photos of the same places now. So people can see the change."

"Ooooh," Maria says. "Now you're talking."

"And then we can present it all with a fun event, but we can use it to create awareness. Then people may commit to continuing to help," I say.

"We can really be like Jeek, and film the event too!" Maria suggests.

"Yes!" I say. "We can put the film on our website too. And show it to classes in our school, and other schools, to teach kids there too."

"Your grandmother will be so proud." Ms. Tremt sighs happily.

Maria and I hit the bookshelves, and the computer, and start to brainstorm. We can raise money for the Marine Conservancy, which is one of the organizations my grandmother worked for. We think about a bunch of fun activities like water balloon fights, dunk tanks, and Slip 'N Slide and agree to pull in some other kids to help think of more ideas. I know I can talk Faris into it.

"We can have an information table at each activity," Maria says.

"Definitely," I agree. "And let's have a 'Dream Team' station."

"What's that?" Maria asks.

"That's your station!" I say. "We can have a whole bunch of art supplies and paper. Then you can help people write stories and draw sketches. We can collect them all and put them together.

It'll be a group work of art that can remind everyone of our cause."

Maria loves that idea, of course. We know we have a lot more work to do, but we can't wait to present the idea to Jada.

"There's no use spending more time on it if she doesn't like it," I say.

"Doesn't like it?" Maria asks. "How can that happen? She's going to love it."

"I think so too," I agree. "But let's not count our nenes before they hatch." (Just a reminder, a nene is a Hawaiian goose, in case you didn't get my little joke. Ha.)

"Agreed," Maria says.

We head to the cafeteria to see if Jada is in there. She is, wrapping up a stack of care packages that the Be the Change club is sending to soldiers overseas.

"Presenting . . . the first project of our subgroup," I announce.

Maria presents the Story of Our WaterWorld idea. I know it's technically *my* idea, but I'd rather listen to her talk than do the talking myself. And anyway, I need to save my voice for comedy.

"Guys, I *love* it!" Jada gushes. "Just make sure not to overextend yourselves. You've got a lot of different things going on, and that's going to take a lot of volunteers. So you might want to cut back a little if you can't get the help."

"Right," Maria says.

"Believe me, I'm speaking from personal experience," Jada says. "And make sure to outline a schedule and a budget right away. You can change it as you come up with more ideas, but you need to know that you have enough time and money to make it work."

"Can we run things by you?" I ask. "I mean, I know you're busy, but seeing as this is our first project and all."

"Of course," Jada says. "Ask me anything . . . except to do the work. I don't have time for that."

"Thanks, Jada," Maria says. "We'll definitely take our time and make sure we think through every detail."

"And every other detail too." I laugh. "We're talking about Maria now."

"I know." Jada laughs. "That's why *she's* in charge!"

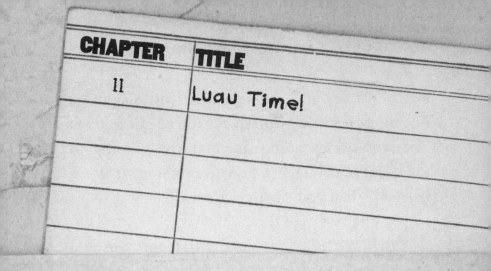

CHAPTER	TITLE
11	Luau Time!

Maria and I are super busy with school and homework and baseball practice and project planning all day on Friday, so we don't get to check in with Ms. Tremt much. We giggle to ourselves when we see her wandering the hallways, looking in air vents and making odd noises. We check in with her at the end of the day. No bird.

I can hardly sleep that night, and wake up before the sun even rises. My stomach is doing flip-flops and my chest is sweaty and feels like it's on fire. I'm not worried about the bird, though, or some time-fabric tear or anything like that at all. I'm freaking out thinking about the comedy contest later. What if I bomb? What if no one laughs? What if I look down and I'm not wearing any pants? Okay, that's not going to happen, because Mom will never let that happen, but I've had some dreams that have turned that image into a big worry on my list.

My cell phone buzzes to tell me I have a new text message.

It's Maria. The day is already off to a good start.

Heading out to meet our friend.

Can I stop by soon?

It's important.

Sure, I text back.

At nine a.m., the doorbell rings and I run down to get it.

"Hi, Maria," Yumi says. "Cute skirt!"

Maria beams at Yumi. "Thanks!" she says.

Maria grabs my arm and starts yanking me out the door.

"Tell Mom I'll be back," I say.

"We need to stop by the mall to pick up an outfit for the contest later," Maria says, which is news to me.

"You're doing that now?!" Yumi yelps. "Mom is going to be so mad. You should have done that a week ago. You know she's going to want you to stay home and practice your routine."

"I know." I laugh nervously.

"That's why *you're* going to tell her," Maria says to Yumi, like a boss.

"He owes me a favor, then," Yumi says.

"I do," I agree. "And let Mom know that Maria's going to help me practice the routine while we shop."

After Yumi closes the door, Maria picks up a few items she has hidden in the bushes, and then we sneak behind the garage. Maria fills me in on the details. Ms. Tremt frantically searched the school late Friday afternoon to no avail. She returned to the library, sure that terrible consequences were awaiting, when she finally found the Hawaiian rail cuddled up in a box of books. So Ms. Tremt brought "Manu" back to her house (that's what she's calling the bird now; it's Hawaiian for . . .

you'll never guess . . . bird) and e-mailed Maria. Maria had gone to the movies with her brothers and didn't check her e-mail until the morning, but as soon as she did, she made plans to meet Ms. Tremt. Maria picked up the bird, and *The Book of Memories*, and even a special gift for Akemi that I'd asked for help with.

When we're out of sight of the house, we sneak behind my garage and activate *The Book of Memories*. Aloha, Hawaii 1900!

Our first job is to take Manu to the secret pond and release him there. Mission accomplished!

"Did you ever wonder why birds are so happy?" I ask Maria.

"I have not," Maria says.

"They eat everything that bugs them," I say.

See? I promised I'd practice.

Next stop: Akemi's. She's so excited when she sees us that she squeals and pulls us into a big group hug.

(Honestly, I never really pictured Akemi as a group-hug kind of girl.)

I'm just as excited as she is when I see that

all of her stuff is right where it belongs, nothing packed up and ready to ship off to Japan.

"Why are you still here?" she says. "Did you lose your job?"

"Oh no," Maria says. "They're still waiting for us on the pineapple plantation."

"They have another boat going there on Tuesday," I fib. "So we decided to stick around so we could go to Leilani and Tua's with you."

"You're making me so happy," Akemi says. "I really wanted to go, but I definitely wouldn't have gone there by myself."

We follow the path past the secret pool, around the beach, and down the hill into the village. Tua was right. It's pretty easy to find their home; it's the noisiest one on the path.

"Aloha!" Tua cries to us from down the road.

He runs up to us and tackles me in a big bear hug. He nearly knocks me over. I think I'm done with hugging for the day.

"This is Makuahine," Tua says, introducing his mother.

Tua's mom places flower necklaces, called leis, around each of our necks.

"Aloha," she says to each of us.

"Nice to meet you," Maria says.

"Thank you for inviting us to your home," I add. "This is incredible!"

Leilani and Tua introduce us to their family, and there are way too many people to keep track of. Aunts and uncles, grandpas and grandmas, and a whole table of cousins: Akamu, Mano, Hiapo, Noelani, Ka Nui, Lalama, Pono . . . you get the picture.

So the first thing I need to tell you about is the food. Because there is literally a ton of it. There's poi, which is made from the mashed-up stems of the taro plant and looks like it could be a food cousin of *okayu*, a Japanese rice porridge. I *love* okayu. Poi, not so much. There's salted fish, which is delish, and a salted jerky that Leilani tells me is called *pipikaula*. The most impressive thing on the menu, though, is the kalua pig. That's right, a whole pig, wrapped in banana leaves, which the family has cooked in an underground oven. We watch as they pull the pig out and shred up the meat. It's juicy and flavorful and I can't eat enough of it. Maria can't eat it, though. She thinks the pig is staring at us.

I'm not even finished with my last bite when Tua pulls me aside. He takes off his shirt and tells me to do the same. I'm a little self-conscious, but it seems like all the guys at the party are doing it, so what have I got to lose? Then some of Tua's cousins come over carrying a pile of grass skirts.

"Put one on," Tua informs me.

"Seriously?" I say.

"Seriously," Tua says.

I know how powerful his bear hugs are, so I put it on without another word.

A group of musicians start pounding their drums, and all the men wearing grass skirts gather in a circle and begin to move to the beat. It's time for the hula, a traditional Hawaiian art form. It uses music and movement to tell a story.

"The Hawaiian goddess Laka divided hula dancers," Tua explains. "The *olapa* are the younger dancers who move with a lot of energy. The *ho'o-paa* are the elders. They sing and play the instruments."

"So we're *olapa*?" I ask.

"You got it." Tua laughs. "Are you ready?"

"Not really," I admit. "But I'll try."

The hula moves are pretty funky. I try to keep up, but I keep getting my feet tangled up in the grass skirt and bumping into the other dancers. Have I mentioned that they're all huge? And they don't look like they're thrilled with my stellar dance moves.

I look over, and Maria, Akemi, and Leilani are pounding the floor, doubled over and laughing hysterically. Very nice, friends, very nice.

The drums start to quiet and one of Leilani's uncles begins to tell a Hawaiian legend.

> *Long, long ago, there were two brother gods known as Kane and Kanaloa. They decided to take a journey and rode a cloud to our beautiful island of Oahu. Kane was a kind and generous god. When his brother began to complain that he was thirsty from the long journey, Kane stopped and looked around. There was no fresh water to drink. Kane used his tall wooden staff*

127

to hit the earth. Immediately, fresh water flowed from the spot. Then the brothers continued on. Every time Kanaloa complained about his thirst, Kane banged the ground with his staff. That is why there are now many water holes between Hanauma and Lae'ahi.

The brothers rested at Ke'apapa Hill. "Brother, can your mighty staff find water here?" Kanaloa teased. Kane stayed quiet and listened to the sound of the water rushing through the hill. He smiled. Instead of banging his staff on the ground, he stomped his foot. Water gushed forth, creating the spring Kapanahou, which has the shape of Kane's foot. The water we have tonight comes from that spring, so we thank you, Kane, for your kindness and generosity.

I'm all wrapped in the story when Maria taps me on the back. I jump, startled. Maria chuckles and points over to a table where Akemi and Leilani are making leis together. They look like they're going to be BFFs. Clearly, our work here is done.

"We're going to have to head off," I tell them. "We have to get ready for the big ship day."

"Oh no!" Leilani says. "We're going to miss you so much!"

It looks like the girls are all starting to tear up, and I want no part of that, so I figure it's time to pull out the surprise.

It's the gift that Ms. Tremt helped me get for Akemi. I hand it to her.

"It's just a small gift," I say. "I hope you'll like it."

Akemi unwraps the present. It's a first-edition printing of Darwin's *On the Origin of Species.*

Of course, Akemi hasn't heard of the book, but she flips through the pages.

"I can't wait to read it," she says. "Thank you."

"I can't wait for you to read it," I say, getting a little emotional myself. "I want you to know how much you mean to me . . . to us."

Look, I'm not a tough guy, but there is no way

I am crying in front of a whole lot of people. And I can tell that I'm just about to cry. It doesn't help that I also have crazy butterflies in my stomach every time I think about the comedy contest that I will be time traveling back to. So it is definitely time to go.

Maria and I wander back to the secret pool. I try out a few of my jokes on her, but she seems to be lost in her thoughts too.

"Going to miss it here?" I ask her.

"I am," Maria says. "It's really a special place."

"I know," I say. "It's always been special to me because it's where many of my family members lived. But this time is different. I can really understand why my uncle works so hard to protect the environment here."

We're ready to go, but we take an extra minute to just sit quietly on the rock and soak in all the awesomeness of the secret pool. Then we activate *The Book of Memories* and I see the space behind my garage. We walk into the picture just in time for . . .

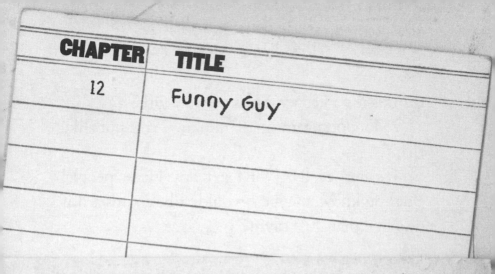

CHAPTER	TITLE
12	Funny Guy

The comedy contest! Maria says good-bye and I head back inside to get changed. Luckily, Maria planned ahead, so she surprised me with a shopping bag with an outfit we had picked out after school during the week. Mom is amused to see me wearing a lei.

"Where did you get that?" she wonders.

"Maria," I say. "She's reading Baba's book, so we've been talking a lot about Hawaii. She asked a florist in town to make me one as a special good-luck charm for the show."

"That was very sweet of her," Mom says. "I

think she's a keeper. She's a lovely girl."

"Mooooommmm," I moan. "It's not like that!"

It's not, really. Don't get any ideas, people! But you know, maybe I wouldn't be so upset if it was like that. Just sayin'.

I could probably win a comedy contest just with a video of the activity in the Mori household right now. Mom would never admit it, because she wants me to think that she's cool as a cucumber, but she's super nervous. I am too. And a Mori-family trait is that when we get nervous, we get flustered and clumsy.

I promise that none of Mom's Satsuma vases will be harmed in the making of this production, but everything else in our house is in danger. Dad can't find his ties, and as he shoves aside clothes in the closet, the tie rack comes flying out and nearly hits me in the head.

"Ken!" Mom yells. "How's he going to win the contest with a concussion? Be careful!"

Then Yumi can't find her lucky socks, and I don't know why *she* needs to be lucky, but there is a whole mess of drama around Yumi's socks. Want to guess where we find them eventually? Yup, in her sock drawer.

"Kai, practice," Mom says as she runs a comb through my hair.

"Mom!" I protest, grabbing the comb. "I can do my own hair. And I've already run through the routine sixteen times today. Let me save my voice."

"I'm sorry," Mom says. "Just remember to hold that beat after you say, 'Did you ever wonder . . .' Don't rush!"

"Yes, Mom." I sigh. "I'll remember."

"And then do that funny thing where you scrunch up your face like you're thinking really hard," Mom adds.

"Already planning on it," I say.

"Oh, and don't forget to leave some space for the audience to react when you finish your line," Mom continues.

"MOM!" Yumi yells. "Enough already!"

We pile into the car. I wish we could say we're packed in like a clown car, but it's not that funny. There are only four of us, and we have a minivan, so we all fit in pretty comfortably.

Dad pulls into the WKBL parking lot where the contest is taking place. There's a check-in table for contestants up front, and Mom pulls me toward it. After I sign in and get my badge and time slot, we head toward the small stage. I'm glad it's small, because it doesn't look so intimidating. The crowd sitting in front of the stage, though? That's intimidating.

"Kai, remember—" Mom starts.

"Mom!" I say. "No more advice! I feel like I'm going to hurl already!"

"Kai-chan," Mom says sternly, to get my attention. "Remember that I love you."

She gives me a kiss on my head and smooths my shirt.

"I love you too," I say.

I wait behind the stage and listen to the girl who's on right before me. She's killing it!

"Please don't bomb. . . . Please don't bomb. . . . Please don't bomb . . . ," I repeat over and over again in my head.

When she's finished, the girl hops down the stairs heading backstage and gives me a high five.

"You were great," I tell her.

"Break a leg," she says.

"And now . . . the comical wonderings of Kai Mori!" a radio-friendly voice announces to the crowd.

I run up the stairs, trying to erase the image that suddenly appears in my head: that I am heading onto a platform where there is a guillotine waiting for me. I get onstage and look around. Microphone, check. No guillotine, thankfully.

I look out and I can't help but smile. The first friendly face I see is Maria's. She totally scammed me and said she had a report to do today. Next to her is Ms. Tremt. Then I see Matt, Jada, Patrick, Jay Kapoor, Jason Miller, Luis, Grace, and pretty much my whole baseball team crowded into the seats up front. I instantly feel a thousand times better.

"Did you ever wonder . . . ?" I start.

[Pause . . . scrunched-up thinking face . . . *Happy, Mom?*]

". . . why we yell 'heads up' to tell someone that they need to duck?"

I see Matt and the other baseball players

think about that one and shake their heads and smile. It's not the big laugh I was hoping for, but I'll take it.

I take a deep breath and continue.

"Did you ever wonder . . . ," I say, "if a cow laughed, would milk come out her nose?"

Jason Miller laughs out loud at that one, and my heartbeat starts to settle down so it doesn't feel like it's going to burst through my chest at any minute.

"Do you ever wonder . . . ," I joke, "why people always say they slept like a baby? Babies cry all night long!"

That one gets even more chuckles. I still have some nerves, but now I feel like they're giving me a boost instead of getting in my way. I look out and pretend that my friends up front are just sitting on the bleachers after baseball practice and I'm joking with them the way I usually do. I channel my nervous energy to rattle off the rest of my set.

"Do you ever wonder . . . ," I ask, "why they don't make mouse-flavored cat food?

"Do you ever wonder . . . why glue doesn't

stick to the inside of the bottle?

"Do you ever wonder . . . what the speed of dark is?"

My timing is getting better. I start to settle into a rhythm, and I feel comfortable enough to move around the stage more, waving my arms and making my gestures more exaggerated to punch up the humor, and trying to make eye contact with different people in the audience. It's a tricky thing, eye contact. Sometimes you look at someone and make a connection right away. They smile back at you and you can tell it helps them connect to you. Other times they look away uncomfortably. When that happens, it can kind of throw you off. But I have a great backup plan. I always turn and look right at my mom next. I know she'll never look away.

"Do you ever wonder . . . why grown-ups say that you're cute as a button? Are buttons really cute?

"Do you ever wonder . . . how much deeper the ocean would be if sponges didn't grow in it?

"Do you ever wonder . . . if swimming is such great exercise to keep trim and fit, then why do whales have so much blubber?"

The crowd is chuckling a lot now, and my friends are starting to get a little loud, the way they do when they're cheering for me when I'm up at bat during our baseball games. It's a great feeling.

"Thank you, Kai Mori!" the announcer calls out when my time is up.

Faris, Matt, Maria, and everyone in my family gather around me after it's over. They're all so excited for me to win, and I hope I don't disappoint them. I'm feeling really good, though. I didn't let my nerves get to me and I did better than I thought I would.

The judges start calling out the contestants in order from last place to first. I feel a sense of relief when my name isn't called in the last-place spot. As the judges keep moving up the list, my nerves start acting up again. I'm not fifth . . . or fourth . . . or third. . . . Could I have actually won this thing?

"Kai Mori," the judge in the middle says. "Second place!"

"First place loser!" I cheer. "I'm the man."

"Kai, that's great for your first stand-up," Mom says encouragingly. "I came in fourteenth my first time!"

"I know, Mom. I'm really happy, honestly," I tell her.

When the judges announce the winner—Mona Myers, the girl who went before me—I cheer louder than anyone. She was really good, and I'm definitely going to hit her up for some advice before we leave.

"I'm so proud of you," Mom says as we head back to the minivan. "Maybe one day when you're a pro, I'll get to see your stand-up at a real comedy club."

"Maybe," I say. "Unless I decide to go into a totally different field."

"Like what?" Mom asks.

"Oh, I don't know," I tease. "Marine biology, maybe?"

"Now, *that's* funny!" Mom laughs.

IF YOU WENT BACK TO HAWAII IN 1900 . . .

If you could actually visit Hawaii in 1900, you could walk through a sugarcane plantation like the one where Akemi worked. The state of Hawaii is made up of eight main islands. Akemi would have traveled more than thirty-five hundred miles to get to Hawaii from Japan. More than two thousand miles away from mainland United States, the city of Honolulu, on the island of Oahu, is one of the most remote cities on the planet.

The Hawaiian Islands are actually the tops of a mountain range that rise up from the floor of the Pacific Ocean. The tallest Hawaiian mountain, Mauna Kea, would be taller than Mount Everest if measured from below sea level and is technically the tallest mountain in the world, from base to top.

Remoteness has made Hawaii a unique place. Because it is such a difficult journey to get to the island (but not by time travel!), Hawaii has the highest percentage of species that do not exist anywhere else on Earth. It also has the highest rate of extinction per square mile. Almost all of the state's native birds are in danger of becoming extinct.

The Hawaiian rail that traveled through the portal with Kai and Maria is an extinct bird species that once lived on the Hawaiian Islands. It was a small, insect-eating bird that lived on the forest floor. It became extinct after people brought new animal species, such as dogs, cats, and mongooses, to the islands. The last individual Hawaiian rails were seen in 1884, but it's possible that one could have existed in 1900.

The first people traveled to the Hawaiian Islands around 400 CE. They came from Polynesian islands like Tahiti and brought their traditions with them. One of those traditions was riding the ocean waves on a longboard—surfing, just like Leilani and Tua! Hawaiians had many chants, legends, and traditions related to surfing. Even the royal family surfed, and many famous Hawaiian chiefs, like Kamehameha I, were known for being excellent surfers. After European missionaries arrived on the islands in the 1820s, they tried to force the Hawaiians to adopt Western culture. Only a few Hawaiians still brought their boards to beaches that were once filled with hundreds of surfers. Surfing began growing in popularity again in the early 1900s, and it is Hawaii's official state sport today.

Queen Liliuokalani was the last Hawaiian ruler of the islands, and when she took the throne in Iolani Palace in 1891, she became the first woman to ever rule Hawaii. Much of the power on the islands, though, had been taken over by rich businessmen and landowners. Liliuokalani fought to restore power back to the royal family, but she lost the battle. In 1898, Hawaii was annexed to the United States, and in April 1900, a provisional government was established. Still, most of the power belonged to the rich landowners and US-based businesses.

Plantation owners recruited workers from China, Japan, Korea, and Portugal. They shaped the population of Hawaii. In 1853, native Hawaiians made up 97 percent of the population. That number fell to 25 percent by 1900, and Japanese immigrants made up 40 percent of the population at that time. Akemi would have been one of thousands of Japanese immigrants working on Hawaiian plantations.

Workers signed three- to five-year contracts. It promised a small amount of money (such as three dollars a month) plus transportation to the island, food, and clothing. Workers had to agree to work twenty-six days a month and ten or more hours a day. If they refused to work or wanted to return home before their contract expired, they would be jailed.

Plantation workers had to plow, chop, and weed sugarcane plants all day long. Plantation managers were strict and made sure that everyone followed the rules. If they didn't, there would be fines or punishment. A worker like Akemi could get in trouble for talking in the fields, or even stretching. Life was so harsh that about half the workers left at the end of their contracts.

After Hawaii officially became a territory of the United States in 1898, these contracts weren't valid any longer. Many workers left the plantations and returned home, but some stayed and looked for new work. The workers who stayed started to strike and fight for their rights. There were twenty-five strikes in the year 1900, and they helped bring the pay rate up to seventy cents a day.

MORE FUN FACTS ABOUT HAWAII

Aloha is the most popular word in the Hawaiian language. It can mean "hello," "good-bye," "welcome," "love," or "best wishes."

Hawaii has the southernmost point in the United States.

Hawaii is the only state where coffee is grown.

The word *Hawaii* means "place of the gods."

Moonwalkers Buzz Aldrin and Neil Armstrong prepared for their moon mission by walking on the lava fields of Mauna Loa.

You could also have met Jacques-Yves Cousteau in the library . . .

The man Kai and Maria met in the library was Captain Jacques-Yves Cousteau, an undersea explorer, filmmaker, inventor, and environmentalist. He invented diving and scuba equipment, as well as a waterproof camera that could film deep undersea. In 1951, he began going on annual trips on his research ship the *Calypso*. He recorded his explorations and used the film to make documentaries and the television show *The Undersea World of Jacques Cousteau.*

Jacques-Yves Cousteau showed millions of people a world that few had ever been able to explore before in person. He also taught people how human activity was destroying the oceans and why it was important for everyone to care about marine habitats and the creatures that live in them. Jacques Cousteau is author of the books *The Silent World, The Shark, Dolphins,* and *Jacques Cousteau: The Ocean World.* He formed the Cousteau Society in 1973, and even though he died in 1997, his environmental work lives on.

If you liked this book,
we're pretty sure you'll like
Billy Sure, Kid Entrepreneur.
Turn the page to read an excerpt
from this fun series!

BILLY SURE
·KID ENTREPRENEUR·

B. SURE

TOP SECRET

INVENTED BY LUKE SHARPE
DRAWINGS BY GRAHAM ROSS

I'M BILLY SURE. YOU'VE PROBABLY HEARD OF me. Wait, that sounds weird, like "Who is this kid and why does he think I've heard of him?" But it's not like that. I mean, I'm not like that. And you probably weren't thinking that anyway because . . . well, like I said, you've probably heard of me. Because I'm *that* Billy Sure, the famous kid entrepreneur, inventor, and CEO of **SURE THINGS, INC.** At the moment I am also the kid who is sitting on a blue couch in a plain little room backstage at the **Better Than Sleeping!** show.

Maybe you will see me on the show tonight, if your parents let you stay up that late on a school night. (If not, maybe you can watch it in your room with the sound turned way down. Just don't get caught—I don't want to be the kid who gets your TV taken away!)

"You're bouncing your legs," Manny tells me. Manny Reyes is my best friend. He is also the chief financial officer of Sure Things, Inc., which is just a fancy way of saying he likes crunching numbers and has a really smart head for business.

I didn't even realize I was doing it. I look at my legs. Reason #35 why Manny is the greatest CFO: He is always right. My knees are definitely bouncing like Ping-Pong balls on a trampoline.

"Don't do that when you're onstage," Manny continues. "It makes you look nervous. Don't pick your nose, either. Or burp. Or throw up. Definitely don't throw up."

"But I *am* nervous. I might throw up," I say.

Manny gets a puzzled look on his face. "Why? You've been on TV before."

"Just the local news. This is national TV. Millions of people will be watching!"

Manny grins. "Exactly. This is a fantastic marketing opportunity. So don't blow it!"

"Way to make me less nervous," I reply, grabbing my knees in an attempt to stop my bouncing legs.

My dad leans forward. He's sitting at the other end of the blue couch. "You'll do great, Billy. We're proud of you. I just wish your mother could be here."

My mom travels a ton, as a scientist doing

research for the government. I don't know much more than that. She's been on assignment for a while now, but she knows all about what's been going on with me because we e-mail a lot.

"Why do *I* have to be here?" my sister, Emily, moans. She hasn't looked up from her cell phone in three hours. "I'm bored, hungry, and thirsty."

"I couldn't just leave you at home while we came to New York, Emily. That'd be illegal," replies my dad.

"I'm fourteen!" she argues, keeping her eyes on her phone. "And very mature for my age. I'm perfectly capable of taking care of myself!"

"Sure you are, Ninja Spider," I taunt her. Lately Emily wears only black. Black shirts, black pants, black shoes, black everything. That's why I've nicknamed her Ninja Spider.

Emily finally looks up from her phone to glare at me. She wipes her blond bangs out of her face. Everyone says we look alike, which is weird because she's a girl. She notices my legs are bouncing again, despite my best efforts to stop them.

"A kangaroo called. He wants his legs back," she says.

Before I can think of a comeback, a can of soda appears in front of Emily's face. "Soda?" someone asks. "I heard you say you were thirsty. In the room across the hall there's a fridge full of free drinks. Stuff to eat, too. Chips. Candy. Fruit, if you're feeling healthy."

Emily, being in a classic Emily mood, takes in a deep breath. I know her well enough to know that when she exhales, she'll snap that she doesn't want a soda; she wants to go home. But before she speaks, she looks up and sees who is holding the can in front of her.

DUSTIN PEELER!

I'm sure you know who Dustin Peeler is too. (See? I don't just say that about myself. Not that I think I'm as famous as Dustin Peeler.) In case you don't know, Dustin Peeler is the most popular teen musician on the planet at the moment. He can sing. He can dance. He can walk on his hands. He can play guitar, piano, drums, English horn, and didgeridoo—upside down.

And according to Emily, he is the most gorgeous human being who ever graced the earth with his presence.

Dustin Peeler smiles his perfect smile, teeth glistening like ocean waves on a sunny day. Emily's mouth drops open, her jaw practically scraping the floor. "Thank you," she manages to squeak out as she takes the can of soda. Her knees begin to shake.

"No problem," he replies.

"Now who's part kangaroo?" I whisper, pointing discreetly to Emily's shaking knees.

But Emily ignores me. She still can't take her eyes off Dustin.

I try again. My sister is seriously making a fool of herself, and I feel like it's my duty to let her know. "Emily," I whisper a little louder this time. "You look really dumb with your mouth hanging open like that!"

And then Dustin Peeler notices me for the first time. "Hey, you're the All Ball dude! That thing is awesome!"

"Thanks," I say.

An assistant sticks her head in. "Dustin, we're ready to do your hair."

"But his hair is already perfect," Emily says like she's in a trance.

"Oh, they're just doing their jobs," Dustin says, smiling another dazzling smile. "Have fun out there!" He gives us a double thumbs-up and leaves. Emily resumes breathing.

"Who was that?" Dad asks.

Emily sighs.

"He said the All Ball was awesome," Manny says. "Maybe we could get him to do an endorsement of some kind. Or even write us a jingle!" Quietly singing, "All Ball, All Ball . . . the only ball you'll ever need," Manny pulls out his phone and taps a note to himself.

I told you Manny has a great head for business. He has a ton of brilliant ideas about how to sell Sure Things, Inc.'s products. Without Manny, I wouldn't have a business, just a bedroom full of inventions. And dirty laundry. And a few hidden candy bars (okay, maybe dozens).

Emily pulls out her phone again and immediately starts texting all her friends that Dustin

Peeler just handed her a can of soda. She even texts a picture of the can. "I'm keeping this can forever," she announces.

"Be sure to rinse it out," Dad says.

I guess it was cool to meet Dustin Peeler. I've never bought any of his songs, but I've certainly heard them. But I am much more excited about the other guest on **Better Than Sleeping!** tonight. Manny spots him first, standing out in the hallway. I see his eyes widen with surprise.

"Hey," he says. "Isn't that the baseball player you like? Carl Somebody? The shortstop?"

"Like" is a slight understatement.

Carl Bourette has been my favorite athlete since I was in kindergarten. I have every Carl Bourette baseball card. Carl Bourette bobbleheads. A nearly life-size poster of Carl Bourette, hanging on my door. I know all his stats. His favorite kind of bat. What he puts on his burgers.

My brain is screaming, "CARL BOURETTE!"

But my mouth is saying nothing. My jaw is hanging open, but no words are coming out. Possibly a little drool, but no words.

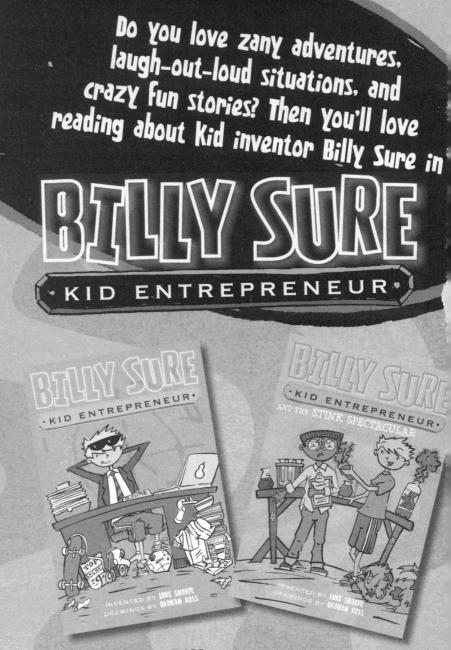